Mrs.

LINDA CHRISTI

in Ireland Hey.

Until It's Time to Die

Ricardo F. Henry

VANTAGE PRESS
New York

FIRST EDITION

All rights reserved, including the right of
reproduction in whole or in part in any form.

Copyright © 1997 by Ricardo F. Henry

Published by Vantage Press, Inc.
516 West 34th Street, New York, New York 10001

Manufactured in the United States of America
ISBN: 0-533-11657-0

Library of Congress Catalog No.: 95-90616

0 9 8 7 6 5 4 3 2 1

In loving memory of my brother Prince;
may his presence bring harmony to the Gods.

1

Alone on the beach where it all began, a lonely man knelt in sadness, listening to the sound of the wind, awaiting the Heavens to pay tribute to an old, familiar soul. A shoal of tiny white doves gathered around him, forming a circle, giving comfort to this troubled man. With tears dripping down his cheeks, his arms opened up toward the sky, he lifted his head up to Heaven and shouted at the top of his voice, "Father! Father! I have seen the light and have beheld in my sight the glory of one of my first loves. I have found the inner part of my soul, binding together the perplexities of my life. She has touched within my heart a soft and tender spot, but I dwell in the depths of sorrow for she loves me not. Father! Father! I was thrilled by her kiss, I was shaken by the sensation of her body, but I do not consider myself a fool; if anything, just a romanticist."

His eyes slowly opened as he contemplated the enigma of life. To a man who has seen the beginning and end of time, a man who has seen the rise and fall of Rome and has even supped with the living God—in retrospect, he sees life as nothing but a cycle of misery and pleasure with death at the end. He recognized that it is not enough for man to survive in the environment in which he lives, for the fulfillment of man's ultimate hope can only be accomplished through his ability to seek wisdom. Yet, at times when man is faced with this challenge, he quivers like a mockingbird hiding from the reflection of its shadow.

He has seen man's reluctance to enjoy the gift of life and pity those who have yet to experience the great awakening, the realization that our entire lives do not follow a path of reality, but rather a stream of delusions that we have convinced ourselves are real. Although he has been part of a race that has shown him anything but kindness, still he is concerned, for there is turmoil amongst the gods. His love and compassion for humanity has transcended all the hatred and bigotry that he had been subjected to by a society that he had been led to believe holds love, values, and integrity in the highest regard.

He smiled to himself as he shivered in cold sweat, for again the spirits of the gods were upon him. He knew they wanted his undivided attention. In a soft and humble voice, he asked, "How long must I be a testimony for the sins of a generation that has long forgotten? What price must I pay to ensure a finite lifestyle that will secure no more immortality?"

Tiny flashes of bright light triggered a playback of memories that rushed through his head like the gigantic screen of a French cinema. He squeezed his head in a futile attempt to suppress the echoes of the voices that roamed through his body like the feet of God trampling all over his tormented soul. He shook his head, clenching his teeth as he remembered the grotesque picture of women and their newborn babies placed upside down over a huge manmade fire. "Burn, burn, burn," chanted by the Egyptians, dressed like monks from a Buddhist monastery, sent him back to reality.

The painful incident that emerged within his consciousness, as if it were yesterday, finally overpowered him and cast him in the sand on the shore. Like a brief psychotic hallucination that often plagues his world, he thought as he regained his composure, knowing that this was part of the price he had to pay for having lived so long.

He continued to kneel in the sand for a few minutes as one by one the tiny white doves departed, and as he rose to his feet a glimpse of a woman running along the shore caught his eyes. Suddenly, an eruption stirred within his soul, triggering a recollection of events that led him to a state of mind deep within himself. His thoughts drifted to the day he met his love.

*   *   *

The sun was beginning to dip behind the hills, creating a breathtaking sunset in Santa Barbara, California. The sunbathers had left, and only a few lovers strolled along the otherwise empty shore.

In isolation, away from the excitement that plagued the seashore, a woman whose eyes were as pretty as the golden flowers of Venice, with movements like an angel riding the wind, lay and watched the sun take its final bow for the day. Her beauty was a delight to every man's eyes, and having loved such a woman would be like a monument inside a man's heart forever. Her skin was soft and smooth, filled with excitement, captivating to the eyes of men as they passed by her, wondering what it would be like to drown themselves in the intriguing fluffiness of her body. Not once did she go unnoticed by those who passed by her that afternoon. She lay there, calm and quite alluring.

She glanced at her watch and was surprised to see how time had flown by. She had been so consumed by the stillness of the ocean and the whistling of the wind that she had not realized that it was time for her to leave if she was going to make it home in time for dinner. She didn't want to see that old familiar look on the chef's face again that said, "ungrateful girl," because she knew how demanding her mother was when it came to meals. Everything had to be perfect.

The sun had been good to her today. She had arrived at the beach at four in the afternoon, and now, only three hours later, she had a beautiful bronze tinge to her complexion. It was particularly noticeable against the white bikini she was wearing.

As she was about to get up, she realized that she was surrounded by three men. They looked at her with an insatiable appetite for her body, an appetite that created a silly smirk on each of their faces. Their intention was obvious, to take her without asking, subjecting her to anything that was necessary in order to fill the cravings that lurked in the darkest regions of their lost souls. She was frightened and rightfully concerned.

She tried to leave but was pushed to the ground by one of the three men. He then held her arms pinned to the ground, while all the time maintaining a very stupid grin on his face. The other two men watched and laughed aloud as if the incident was nothing but a sideshow designed only for their amusement. The laughter ceased as one of the two spectators ripped her bathing suit apart, while his friend continued to keep her pinned to the ground. He was overcome with anticipation, for he knew he was about to enter the gate of heaven without having to have faced death. But before he could penetrate the woman's most private part, he was angered, for he had ejaculated all over himself.

His friend laughed at him. "Damn, boy, you're supposed to wait till you get in before you do that! Here, let me show you how it's done; hold her hands."

During the transition, the woman got one of her hands free and scratched one of her attackers in the face. He slapped her twice. "You like it rough? Then I'll give it to you rough, bitch."

He was interrupted by the shadow of a man who stood in silence between two dogs with fiery looking eyes. Two of the men turned to the stranger while the other continued to keep the woman pinned to the ground. "What can we do for you, nigger?" asked one of the men. The stranger remained quiet; he had a blunt look on his face, one they were unable to read.

"I am warning you, you better move along before you get hurt." The two men went inside their pockets and came back out with switchblades. Still, the stranger remained silent and immovable. The two men moved slowly towards the stranger, whose feet were like concrete in the ground. Suddenly, lightning flashed across the sky and thunder started to roar, getting louder and louder the nearer the men got to the stranger. "Shit, feels like a hurricane out here," said one. Another raised his hand to stab the stranger, only to have the hand severed from his body by a bolt of lightning. He fell to the ground in a screaming frenzy, pointing to the mangled remains of his hand, while the rest of the hand lay several feet from him.

4

"I'm gonna kill this sucker now! Look what you did to my boy!" yelled the other friend as he charged toward the stranger, the switchblade in his right hand ready for the plunge. The third man continued to keep the woman nailed to the ground.

"*Sala majew!*" said the stranger. As if commanded to action, the two dogs leapt in the air towards their master's attacker, knocking him to the ground. The stranger watched as the man struggled for his life, kicking and crying like a child.

The third man released the girl and began staring at the stranger with a terrified look in his eyes. He was shaking all over because he knew it was his turn. "Please mister, don't kill me. I wasn't gonna hurt her; I was just following my friends," he pleaded as he reached in his waist, pulled out a gun, and raised it toward the stranger's head. "Okay, let's see who's in charge now. Stand back, or I'm gonna blow your head off!"

The stranger did not move, just stared at the man. Mesmerized by the stranger's glare, the third man found himself struggling against some unknown force to keep his hand steady as he held the gun. He kept struggling to keep the gun pointed at the stranger, but some force kept turning his hand in the opposite direction. Against his will, he was now pointing the gun at his own head. He tried to move his finger from the trigger, but it was as if his finger was stuck. Realizing what was happening, he closed his eyes and started a silent prayer as he waited to enter eternity.

The stranger walked up to the man and with a gentle tone said, "Give me the gun before anyone else gets hurt; take your friends and go." The stranger took the gun from the man, who stood there as if frozen with his empty hand still pointed toward his own head. The man tried to speak, but no words would come. Finally words came. "You mean you're not going to hurt me, too?"

The stranger shook his head. "In health, all men are tyrants who seek to rule in the world, yet in pain they are like babies in search of their mother's breast," the stranger said as he walked away from the man and over toward the woman.

Relieved, the man ran over to help his friends. He came first to the one bitten by the dogs. He was lying in a fetal position, his hands covering his face. The friend cried out, "Don't kill me! Please don't!"

"It's only me, man. We've got to get the hell out of here because this nigger's going crazy!" He helped his friend to stand and they both hobbled over to the other one.

The man with the mangled hand had lost so much blood that he was going in and out of consciousness. His friends picked him up like a sack of rice and hurried toward their pickup truck, which was parked farther down the beach. They knew they had to get him to a hospital immediately, but explaining what had happened was going to be another story because they knew nobody would believe them.

The stranger knelt down to console the woman. She became alarmed when she turned and stared into the face of a Black man. She thought, *now I am surely doomed; he is just going to finish what the other guys started. But why would he save me from them? Ah, I get it. To have me for himself.* "If you come any closer I'm going to scream my head off," she said.

"I won't hurt you," said the stranger as he attempted to cover her exposed body with a towel that was next to her. She relaxed a little when she noticed a calmness in his eyes and in his gentle manner. Soon she was no longer petrified.

His piercing eyes penetrated her mind and his heart became heavy, for he could see that her perception of his kindness was clouded by the ignorance that has so frequently laid the groundwork for prejudice and discrimination. The stranger knew that her mind was not at ease, for she had never been alone with a Black man before. In her mind the color of his skin symbolized everything that her parents stood against. Although he knew her thoughts, it did not matter.

She soon was composed and he felt it was time for him to leave. He walked several feet away from her, stopped, turned around, stared at her for a brief moment as she stood there trembling. She was puzzled, for she could not understand how it was possible for a man to say so much by saying so little. He smiled at her, then continued on his journey as she watched him walk away without remembering to thank him.

2

The next morning, Monique joined her parents for breakfast. She was still shaken from the previous evening's incident, but tried to put up a cheerful front so that her parents wouldn't worry about her so much. She was their only child, and they would do anything to protect her. Monique was grateful to be back in her world of wealth and power.

During breakfast, her parents listened intently as she re-lived the awful beach incident for the third time. She had told her parents about the incident immediately upon arriving home from the beach. Her father had immediately called up the police chief, and within minutes six patrol cars were at their front door. So she had to repeat the incident all over to complete strangers.

"I can't imagine something like that could happen in our neighborhood!" said Mrs. Ryan.

"I only hope the cops catch the creeps real soon because they sure wouldn't want me to search for them," intoned Mr. Ryan.

His wife and daughter looked at him with a plea because they knew he could be ruthless if put to the test. After all, over the years they had played host to a stream of his "business" associates, some of unsavory reputation.

"Good morning, Mr. and Mrs. Ryan," said Paul as he walked into the dining room unannounced. He was probably one of the few people who could do that. Perhaps the Ryans afforded him this liberty because they felt the attorney-client privilege extended to all his contacts with them, no matter how innocuous. And therefore, if he overheard anything that wasn't really intended for his ears, he simply could not repeat it. Mr.

Ryan had politely brought that to Paul's attention many years before when he'd accidentally walked into the living room while Mr. Ryan was in a private business meeting.

"Good morning, Paul," replied Mr. and Mrs. Ryan in unison.

Paul looked at Monique and said, "You look as lovely as always." Without responding to Paul's gesture, Monique asked to be excused from the breakfast table. Paul felt slighted by her quick exit. "I know I am not exactly one of her favorite persons, but she usually at least says hello. What's wrong with her this morning?"

"She was attacked and almost raped by three men yesterday. Those brutes need to be lynched by their balls," responded Mrs. Ryan.

"I'm sorry. Will she be alright?"

"She is a Ryan, a survivor. Indeed, she will be just fine," replied Mrs. Ryan.

"You said she was almost raped? How did she escape?" Paul asked.

"She was saved by a colored man."

Mr. Ryan interrupted, "I sure would like to thank that boy for rescuing my little girl from those creeps, but I doubt we'll ever meet him."

"According to Monique, he was quite handsome for a colored man," remarked Mrs. Ryan.

"Monique calling a colored man handsome! She must have been really shaken up by the entire ordeal," replied Paul.

"What brings you out here so early in the morning, Paul?" asked Mr. Ryan.

"I have some papers for you to sign, sir."

"I'll be right with you. Would you like some breakfast in the meantime?" asked Mr. Ryan.

"No sir, I've already eaten. Thank you all the same."

Mr. Ryan stopped chewing his food upon hearing Paul's response to his question. He stared at Paul briefly. Paul knew what it meant to be stared at in such a fashion, for he had seen that look several times before.

"Well, maybe just a bite, sir."

Mr. Ryan continued chewing his food. After they had breakfast, Mr. Ryan signed the papers. On his way out, Paul saw Monique kneeling by the pool, running her hand back and forth in the water. Her thoughts were of the stranger who'd rescued her from the three thugs on the beach. She could not find the peace she'd had before the incident.

"I heard what happened. Are you okay?"

She was startled by Paul's words and a disturbing look was on her face as she turned to look up at him.

"I am sorry; I did not mean to sneak up on you like this," said Paul.

"Yes, I am fine," she replied.

"Can I get you anything?"

She could see that for once Paul was not his usual obnoxious self. He was really trying to be sincere. "I'll be alright; I just need to be by myself for a while," said Monique.

Paul turned to leave but stopped when Monique asked, "Can you admire and resent someone at the same time?"

"I didn't realize that you admired me at all," replied Paul.

Monique forced a smile. "No, not you, silly."

"Oh, I take it you are talking about your Mr. Lancelot!"

Monique became serious once again.

"The philosophers had a saying about that," said Paul.

"What's that?" asked Monique.

"They say he who admires and resents you at the same time will assist in carrying your cross, but only to watch your crucifixion." His words caused tears to come to her eyes and once again sincerity echoed in his voice. "I have known you for a long time; never have I seen you so distraught. Now, what's really bothering you, Monique?"

She wiped the tears from her eyes as she explained the reason behind her misery. "He risked his own life to save me from those jerks and all the time I was hating him for even being close to me. I gazed in his eyes, his gentle eyes, and I could see that he knew how I felt about him. Despite that he made sure I was alright. I hate myself for being like this, for not even thanking him. Deep inside I just couldn't bring myself to accept the fact that I was beholden to him. What type of person am I, Paul?"

"A good person who is experiencing what my shrink calls cognitive dissonance."

"What the hell is that? And since when do you see a shrink?"

"It's a long story, but he said when people display major inconsistencies between their behavior and attitude, they become troubled."

"I don't understand," interrupted Monique.

"How do you feel about Black people?"

"I don't hate them, but I think they should stay in their places."

"Would you tell a Black person that he is not in his proper place should he step out of bounds?"

Monique answered quickly, "Yes, I would."

"So your behavior would be consistent with your attitude towards Blacks who step out of bounds or lose their place. But for once you were placed in a position where this was not the case. Your behavior toward the Black man who saved you was not consistent with the way you were raised to feel about him. Frankly, you couldn't and still can't decipher this man."

"You must have a very good shrink."

"For the money I am paying him, he better be good." Paul leaned over and tried to kiss her but she pulled away quickly.

"Don't. Why do you always spoil any chance of us becoming friends?"

"Maybe it's because I want more from you than that."

"Well, I am afraid that's all you are going to get," said Monique as she stormed toward the house.

Paul left the Ryans' feeling rejected once again, a feeling he had grown accustomed to over the years.

*   *   *

Upstairs in her room, Monique lay across the bed wondering whether she should go out looking for the stranger. She

11

only wanted to say thanks, but what if he thought she was trying to come on to him? Better leave well enough alone. Her thoughts were interrupted by a soft tap on the door.

"Who's there?"

"It's only me, Ms. Monique," said Benjamin, the butler. "I wanted to let you know Ms. Charlene is downstairs waiting to see you."

The sound of Charlene's name brought a smile to Monique's face. She and Charlene had been best friends since kindergarten. They had done everything together and told each other their darkest secrets. She'd thought Charlene wasn't arriving back from Paris for another day. "Benjamin, tell her I'll be down in a jiffy."

Monique was anxious to hear about Charlene's trip to Paris. It would take her mind off her nightmare for a while. Charlene was a free spirit and always had some bizarre encounters to relate.

Monique walked into the living room. "Mon ami!" said Charlene in her best imitation of the French, as they embraced and kissed each other on both cheeks. They then sat together on the couch.

"When did you get back from Paris?"

"Yesterday."

"Did you bring back half of Galeries Lafayette with you?" asked Monique, jokingly.

"To hell with Galeries Lafayette! Child, let me tell you, I met this guy at a nightclub called La Palacé. He was something else on the dance floor and even better under the sheets."

"Charlene, you are too much."

"This guy sure knows how to romance a woman. He took me to the Louvre, cruising down the Seine, a stroll up the Eiffel Tower, and to top it all, proposed to me at a small cafe in Opera Square! Of course you know I have been to all those spots a zillion times, but I just played along as if it was my first trip to Paris."

"So when is the wedding?"

"Child, please. The only thing I want from a man is that muscle between his legs. So what's new with you? Anything interesting happen while I was away?"

"Oh, nothing much. Yesterday I went for my usual rest on the beach and almost got raped by three men."

Charlene looked startled for a moment, then started laughing.

"You almost got me there," she said, then stopped laughing as abruptly as she started when she realized that this was not one of her friend's usual pranks. This was real serious stuff. "Wait a minute, you are serious. Did they hurt you?"

"No, they didn't hurt me—thanks to a colored man who I then shunned in a disgraceful manner."

"I see," said Charlene, with a grin returning to her face. "So that's what that look is, guilt?" She could read her best friend so well.

"It's not funny, Charlene. I have been feeling like a real horrible person since yesterday. Later I am going for a walk on the beach. Maybe I will run into him, though I doubt it."

"See that you are not alone."

"Don't worry. Dad has already asked Jimmy to accompany me."

"Jimmy? Your dad sure must mean business because that man would scare King Kong himself. Though I am surprised your father didn't call out the marines."

"Don't worry, he nearly did. Mom and I had to do everything to restrain him. But he succeeded in getting out nearly half the police force."

Monique and Charlene talked for hours about their favorite subjects: men, shopping, and travel. Before long, morning appeared to have suddenly turned into evening. The women said their goodbyes and Charlene left for the cottage she occupied by herself at one corner of her parents' estate. Charlene liked her privacy and couldn't stand her parents butting into her life. So a year before she'd moved into the cottage that for years had been used as guest quarters. This way she was close enough to enjoy her parents' money and still live as she chose.

Monique was walking on the beach with Jimmy several feet behind her. She gazed all around, hoping that she would see the man who had saved her from a tragic fate. Her search was proving futile, so she ceased and took sanctuary on a cool part of the shore. Her eyes caught Jimmy staring at her in a lustful manner. She ignored his stare, for she knew he would not dare say what was on his mind. To do so would cause him great discomfort.

Soon, the dazzling of the sun gave way to the serenity of the darkness. Monique and Jimmy walked back to the house. She was disappointed for she knew its meaning: having to bear another day the guilt of not having thanked the stranger. Monique went to her room as Jimmy was called away by Mr. Ryan.

"Any signs of those bastards who attacked my daughter, Jimmy?"

"No sir, we had no problem."

"If anyone goes close to her, kill the son of a bitch, then ask questions later. Do you understand?"

"Yes sir."

The following morning at the breakfast table, Mr. Ryan informed Monique that he had hired another bodyguard by the name of Nick. He was to take turns with Jimmy in order to ensure her safety wherever she went.

"Father, don't you think you are overdoing it a little?"

"Of course not! You're my only child and I'll be damned if I am going to let anything happen to you."

A few hours after breakfast, Monique decided to take an early jog on the beach. She was startled by a musclebound three-hundred-pound man who appeared out of nowhere to introduce himself.

"Who the hell are you?"

"I am Nick," replied the man in a very deep voice.

"That you are," said Monique sarcastically after looking at him from head to toe for a few seconds as she continued to jog toward the beach.

She jogged for about a mile on the beach, then stopped when she saw Nick begin to look as if he was about to have a cardiac arrest. "Now how do you expect to be my gallant knight if you can't keep up with me?" asked Monique with a smile on her face.

Nick, with his head almost between his knees gasping for air, answered "I didn't know the job would be so hazardous to my health." They both laughed. "Besides, I wasn't planning on running anybody to their death," Nick said, creating even more laughter between the two.

Her laughter quickly turned to seriousness and for a moment she thought her eyes were deceiving her. "It's him, it's him," she whispered to Nick. Nick pulled out his revolver. "What are you doing? Put that away," said Monique.

"I thought . . . wasn't he one of the men who attacked you?"

"Are you crazy? If it were not for him I would probably be dead."

Monique tried to explain to Nick what had happened two days before, while the stranger sat on the beach looking out into the ocean. He was not wearing any shirt. She recognized his two white German shepherds, one on each side of him, facing the ocean as well. It was a strange scene as she and Nick watched the three of them sit there with their eyes closed, looking as if they were monks at peace with the universe.

"I have never seen dogs sleep sitting up like that before," said Nick.

"That's because they are not sleeping, Nick."

"So what are they doing?"

"Looks as if they are in a trance or something, almost like a meditative state," replied Monique. Monique was quiet for a while, trying to decide whether or not to approach the stranger. Eventually she got enough courage and went over to him.

"Hello there, remember me?" she said.

The stranger did not respond. The dogs, with their eyes still closed, were also unresponsive.

"I hope I am not disturbing you and your friends. Hello, remember me?" she said with a big smile on her face. After a time, the stranger spoke.

15

"Sit down and listen." She slowly sat beside him and his dogs while gazing at his eyes, which were still closed.

"What are you listening to?" she asked. A minute ticked by before he responded.

"We are listening to the stories of the ocean that we may one day share them with a generation of unbelievers, like yourself, who have yet to experience the symphony of life."

She did not know what he was trying to say and felt uncomfortable talking to him with his eyes closed. "Do you always talk with your eyes closed?" she asked.

A few seconds went by again, then he answered. "When I close my eyes, I am in the realm of the gods, but when I open them, so often I find myself in the presence of Lucifer's paradise."

"I promise you that if you open them you won't be disappointed. Besides, you don't even know who I am." She was surprised when he described her completely without missing the butterfly, a small tattoo on the inner side of her right thigh. She was impressed with his recollection of the near tragedy that created their first encounter.

His eyes and those of his two dogs opened simultaneously. Both dogs went and sat behind Monique. Monique became concerned. "Do these guys behind me know that we are pals?" she asked.

"They are as much a part of you as you are of them."

"Thank you."

"For what?"

"For the other night."

"To have done otherwise would have meant a cancelled destiny."

"I am afraid I don't understand."

"You are welcome," said the stranger without explaining what he meant.

The stranger got up, and once again his dogs simultaneously got up with him. "It was nice talking to you. Stay well," he said. He began to walk away.

16

"Would you like to come to a party at my home tonight?" asked Monique.

"I would love to."

"I don't even know your name," she said.

"David, David Sebastein."

She started, "I am—" but he interrupted her sentence before she completed by adding, "Monique Ryan." Her mouth opened wide as she wondered how he knew her name. She gave him directions and her address before each bid the other farewell, not knowing that he knew where she lived before she'd even told him.

Monique arrived home and hurried toward her mother, who was partway down the stairs. Her mother noticed that she was projecting her usual vivacious aura, which had seemed to have disappeared of late.

"My, you look like someone back to her old self again," said Mrs. Ryan.

"I have wonderful news, mother!"

"Oh, pray tell, what could this be? The last time you had wonderful news it almost sent us bankrupt."

"Seriously, mother."

"Okay my child, tell me all about it," she said to Monique as they walked down the remaining two steps and sat on a nearby chair in the living room.

"I have invited Sebastein to our party tonight."

"You know he is welcome if he is a friend of yours."

"You don't understand, mother: this is the man who helped me get away from those creeps who attacked me the other day."

Mrs. Ryan's eyes bulged out of her head like a cartoon character; she began to hyperventilate as she held her chest. She finally caught her breath and responded. "You invited the colored man to tonight's party?"

"Yes, I did. He is quite nice, actually."

Mrs. Ryan was worried about what her husband might think. "Good heavens! Who is going to tell Avery?"

"Why, you of course, mother," said Monique as she got up and went upstairs to her bedroom, leaving her mother in a daze.

17

Shortly she was on the phone with Charlene. "Charlene, you will never guess who I ran into on the beach."

"No doubt it's a man from the sound of your voice."

"Yes, it is a man, but it's not what you think."

"Oh, that's too bad."

"The man who rescued me from those three thugs is coming over tonight!"

The sound of Charlene swallowing hard could be heard miles away. "You did say he was Black, didn't you?" Charlene asked, a little shocked because this was uncharacteristic for Monique. Risqué things like this were usually Charlene's forte.

"That's right and he is coming over tonight."

"Child, your father will never allow it, not in a million years."

"Mother already promised to work on him."

"Work on him! She better be willing to do much more than that. Over his dead body is more in line with reality." They both laughed as they continued their conversation for a few more minutes before hanging up.

Monique could hear her parents shouting at the top of their voices. She knew that her mother was having a tough time convincing Mr. Ryan that it was alright to play host to Sebastein for one night. The shouting continued for about thirty minutes, then things began to quiet down.

Monique opened her door slightly and peeped down the hallway only to see mother walking toward her. "Mother, is it alright?" she whispered aloud. Mrs. Ryan stopped for a second and winked at her. Monique knew that wink was an indication that her mother had won again. Monique went back inside her room, threw herself across the bed, and stared at her closet, trying to figure out what to wear to the party. She wanted to be particularly stunning tonight.

3

The Ryans' guests started to make their entrances at 9:00 P.M. The guest list consisted of senators, judges, diplomats, bankers, even top-ranking mobsters. Anybody who was somebody was there. It was a group of people whose wealth amongst them could quite possibly have stopped world hunger.

Eleven thirty and still there was no sign of Monique's guest. An anxious 25-year-old lady, dressed in red, was beginning to doubt if he would ever show up.

"Still no sign of him?" asked Charlene.

"No. Maybe he couldn't make it," replied Monique.

While they were talking, Benjamin, a 65-year-old Caucasian male, answered the door bell. He was taken aback when he opened the door and saw a tall, well-dressed Black man standing there, something he had never seen in all his years of being the Ryans' butler.

"I am sorry, sir, but I do believe you are at the wrong residence," said Benjamin in a slow, sluggish voice.

"This is the Ryans' residence, is it not?"

"Indeed sir, it is," replied Benjamin snobbishly.

"Then would you be good enough to tell Ms. Monique Ryan that David Sebastein is here?"

Benjamin looked the visitor over again, then said, "Do wait by the door if you will." He slammed the door as he sauntered to the ballroom to locate Monique.

Sebastein stood at the door and waited patiently. Over the years he had become used to the ignorance. The door soon opened again and this time it was Monique greeting Sebastein with more appropriate pleasantries.

"Hope I didn't keep you waiting long."

Sebastein shook his head indicating "no" as she took him by the arm and escorted him toward the ballroom. As they crossed the entrance into the ballroom, all eyes watched in awe. The orchestra had begun to play "Strangers in the Night." The sight of the couple created quite a stir among the guests.

Ignoring the stares and whispers, Monique took Sebastein over to introduce him to her parents. They tried their best to give the impression that they were pleased with his presence, but their inner thoughts were transparent. Still, he understood the nature of their ways.

"We wish to thank you, Mr. Sebastein, for coming to the aid of our daughter the other day," said Mrs. Ryan.

"I was just at the right place at the right time," replied Sebastein.

"Luckily for us," interjected Mr. Ryan.

"And whom do we have here?" Charlene interrupted.

"Charlene, this is Sebastein, the gentleman who rescued me on the beach."

"Aren't you a knight in shining armor," Charlene said as she winked at Sebastein and took a sip from her glass.

Sebastein, smiling politely, seemed distracted by a couple a distance away, the Russian ambassador and a beautiful Russian girl, Natasha Towasky. The ambassador looked around as if to see who was nearby, then he leaned over and whispered to Natasha, "The nicest thing about Russia is that he would never be allowed to attend a party like this."

With all the chatter, mixed with the sound of the orchestra, Natasha barely heard what the ambassador was saying. Besides, she was trying to check out the younger males in the room.

Upon hearing the ambassador's comment, Sebastein, who was about twenty feet away at the time, left the Ryans and Charlene and walked over to the ambassador. Sebastein walked up to the couple just in time to catch Natasha's champagne glass as it fell out of her hand. Her drink did not even spill. Natasha gasped and the ambassador looked up, both startled not only by Sebastein's sudden presence but also by the swiftness of his hand. Sebastein slowly handed Natasha her drink as she accepted reluctantly, still baffled by what had transpired.

Sebastein then turned to Nicholas Pavlov, the Russian ambassador, and said, "The essence of a man's thought will always bear testimony to his way of life; the eradication of any social disease must begin with the elimination of a twisted mind. For a man who has to convince himself that he's better or stronger than others is the weakest of all men. Good night." Without another word, Sebastein turned and walked away, returning to Monique, whose heart was about to leap out of her chest as she wondered what on earth Sebastein had said to the couple.

"He must have heard you," said Natasha to Nicholas Pavlov.

"Impossible!" replied Nicholas with a puzzled look on his face.

"Would you give me the pleasure of this dance?" Sebastein asked Monique, who by this time was standing by herself. She appeared surprised by his question. Rather than giving him an answer immediately, she looked around the room at the other couples dancing. Sebastein saw her hesitation and understood her reason.

"On second thought, maybe we shouldn't."

"Nonsense, I would love to," replied Monique.

As Sebastein and Monique made their way onto the dance floor, couples started to step aside as if to give them room. They were both light on their feet as they danced to the melodies of the orchestra. They moved with the grace and style of Fred Astaire and Ginger Rogers. Sebastein and Monique gazed into each other's eyes, oblivious to the fact that they had become the center of attention, being the only couple left on the dance floor.

Suddenly, at the top of his voice, Sebastein put words to the tune of the orchestra. His powerful voice emulated the echo of Mario Lanza and Luciano Pavarotti rolled in one. He glanced at the conductor of the orchestra, who smiled in approval. The music soon came to an end, as it was break time for the players, who had been going nonstop for the past hour and a half. Sebastein and Monique stopped dancing and were greeted with the applause of the entire room. Sebastein stepped away from Monique and bowed to her, she reciprocated, then he bowed to the conductor of the orchestra. For that brief moment, Sebastein was not seen as a Black man, but as a tenor with a powerful voice who had bridged the gap between the two worlds.

"You are quite a singer," said Paul as he walked up to join Sebastein and Monique.

"Sebastein, this is Paul Grayson, the family's attorney."

"Thank you, Mr. Grayson," replied Sebastein.

"You're one hell of a singer," said Charlene as she joined the group.

"Thank you, you're very kind," replied Sebastein.

"I am anything but kind," replied Charlene as she held Sebastein's arm.

"Charlene, you look as sensuous as always," said Paul.

"Why, thank you, Paul. But then again you find anything in a skirt sensuous," replied Charlene. Monique giggled as Paul tried to reintegrate his ego.

"I just love a woman with fire in her blood, don't you, Sebastein?"

Sebastein hung his head instead of answering Paul.

"Oh, so if not a fiery woman, what types turn you on?" asked Paul as he directly faced Sebastein.

"That's enough, Paul," said Monique.

"It's okay," interjected Sebastein and then he turned to Paul and said, "My woman must be able to bear the fruit of a king and drink the wine from a vine that only angels can swallow."

"She sounds like quite a woman. The question is, does such a woman exist?" asked Paul.

"Indeed, I have already found her," said Sebastein as he stared at Monique.

His words and action left Charlene's mouth wide open and a look of disbelief on Paul's face. Monique was quite flabbergasted, not only by Sebastein's words but by the message that was being sent by his eyes. She caught her breath, then tried to get Sebastein away before he was bombarded with more questions. "Excuse me, I am going to show Sebastein around."

"It was nice meeting both of you," said Sebastein as he and Monique departed.

They strolled outside on the grounds for about five minutes, in silence, each indulging in private thoughts. Monique was wondering what Sebastein had meant by his last comment to Paul.

"We're even," said Sebastein, finally breaking the silence.

"What do you mean?"

"You rescued me from your friends, and I rescued you from the three men; that makes us even."

Monique laughed. "They are harmless, really, Charlene is my best friend, a little wild I must admit. Paul . . . well, Paul . . ."

"Paul is in love with you," said Sebastein, completing her sentence. Sebastein stopped walking, and his face suddenly became tense as his eyeballs shifted back and forth in his head like those of a little boy watching a Ping Pong tournament.

"What's wrong?" Monique asked, a little concerned by his sudden silence.

"Someone is following us."

Monique looked around; there was no one in sight. "These grounds are safe, don't worry," she said in a comforting tone.

Sebastein walked a few feet from Monique, his fist clenched as he whispered, "Show yourself." His words, like a magnet, brought a man hurling from the bushes into the open as if someone had thrown him out by force. They got closer to the man only to discover who it was.

"Nick, what are you doing?" asked Monique angrily.

"Your father wanted me to keep an eye on you," replied Nick as he slowly got up from the ground, holding his head.

"A friend of yours?" asked Sebastein.

"My great protector is more like it. Nick, do us both a favor and go back to the house," said Monique.

"I am sorry, but your father said . . ."

"Don't be sorry, just do it," replied Monique. Nick left reluctantly.

"I am sorry. I really didn't know," said Monique.

"The duties of a caring father do not need an excuse or an apology."

"Maybe we should start to head back to the house," said Monique. Sebastein nodded in agreement.

They started back toward the house and continued to share tidbits about themselves. Although Monique thought Sebastein was a bit eccentric, she knew she wanted to see him again.

"How about joining me at another party tomorrow night?" Monique asked.

"Another party! I don't know if these old bones can take it."

"Old! You don't look a day over thirty."

Sebastein laughed. "That's sweet of you to say but I am thirty-nine."

"I still say you don't look a day over thirty. Anyway, I know Charlene would like you to come. She's the one giving a pool party tomorrow, and believe me it will be a pool party. There will be lots of girls in bikinis doing all kinds of unimaginable things in the water."

"I don't even own swim trunks."

"Then I am afraid you'll just have to wear your birthday suit." They both laughed aloud.

Sebastein walked her to the door, and as he extended his hand to shake hers he said, "Thank you very much for an enchanting night."

She slipped a piece of paper with her telephone number and Charlene's address in Sebastein's extended hand, leaned over slightly and brushed his cheek with a kiss. "The pleasure was all mine."

"Good night, and remember to extend my gratitude to your parents for being the gracious hosts."

"I will," said Monique as she closed the door with a big smile on her face. She hurried to her room because she wanted to savor the moment all by herself.

The following morning, Monique was awakened by the telephone. She almost knocked off the lamp trying to get to it, hoping that it would be Sebastein.

"Hello." She tried to sound awake.

"You guys had too much fun last night. Ah, where did you two lovebirds disappear to?"

"Oh, Charlene, it's you. Don't you think it's too early in the morning?"

"Thanks a lot. Well, did he kiss you?"

Monique yawned aloud, replying, "No. If you must know, Charlene, he was a perfect gentleman."

"Child, when it comes to sex, men don't know the first thing about being gentlemen. Sure they'll pretend, but they are like animals just waiting in the bushes, just waiting for the right moment. Don't keep me in suspense, what did you do?"

"Nothing, Charlene, but talk."

"I noticed he has an accent; where is he from?"

"You know, I didn't even ask him. I invited him to your party tonight. I hope it's alright."

Meanwhile, several miles away from the Ryans' residence, in another huge mansion, an elderly man in his sixties, dressed in traditional Egyptian garments, humbled himself to his master. The elderly man had been a guardian and a friend to the Egyptian prince through timeless eras. Once again the elderly man found himself troubled by the limitation of his master's time. He watched his master, who was sitting in the midst of the garden in meditation, wondering whether or not he should interrupt. "Master, master," said the elderly man in a soft voice.

Sebastein opened his eyes and focused his attention on a man who had proven his love and loyalty so many times. "Alimar, my good friend," said Sebastein as he rose to his feet.

"Is she the one, master? Is she the one?" asked Alimar.

"Yes, Alimar, she is the one," replied Sebastein, resting his hand on his old friend's shoulders.

"Do not concern yourself, master. I have never failed you and I never will."

25

"I know," said Sebastein as he kissed Alimar on the forehead. Sebastein then walked away, leaving Alimar with a renewed sense of hope. Sebastein took his two German shepherds and headed toward the gate. He was taking the dogs for a mid-morning walk.

Back at the Ryans' residence, Monique had just strolled downstairs after a wonderful night's rest. Her mother was sitting in the den reading a book. As Monique passed by, Mrs. Ryan looked up and said, "Your guest was a smash at the party last night, and you seemed to get along with him."

"Does that mean you approve, mother?"

"Approve of what?"

"Our friendship, of course."

"Your father and I have agreed that he seems like a nice enough fellow, but see that it doesn't go beyond anything but friendship."

"Oh mother, you both worry too much," said Monique with a shrug of her shoulders.

"Do we?"

"By the way, mother, will you be coming to Charlene's party?"

"I should say not. My back is still recovering from her last one."

The doorbell rang and Monique hurried to answer it. She opened the door to see two men dressed in uniforms and two vans behind them with "Gloria's Florist" on the sides.

"We have a delivery for a Ms. Monique Ryan," said one of the delivery men.

"I am she."

"Great. If you will wait right here we will have your deliveries out in a few minutes," said one of the delivery men. The two men hopped back into their vans, then came out with beautiful arrangements of flowers. After several trips back and forth to their vans, they had filled the Ryans' living room with sixteen different arrangements of beautiful flowers. The living room was suddenly turned into a Garden of Eden. Monique was speechless.

After the delivery men left, Mrs. Ryan came into the living room to see what all the commotion was about.

"Look, mother, they are for me."

"For you? But who are they from?"

Monique held her chest. "I haven't looked at the card yet."

"Well, child, don't just stand there. Open the card!"

Monique opened the card and the smile on her face became even bigger.

"Are you going to tell me or not?" asked Mrs. Ryan.

"Oops. Sorry, mother. They are from Sebastein." Monique read the card aloud to her mother. " 'Monique, I trust that when these flowers are in your company, they will become even more beautiful after being graced by your presence,' signed Sebastein." With his telephone number at the bottom of the card.

Mrs. Ryan became very serious. "They must have cost a small fortune—but remember what your father and I said," commented Mrs. Ryan as she walked away.

Monique stood there for a few minutes and enjoyed the flowers before going upstairs to her room to call Sebastein. Alimar answered the phone and called Sebastein.

"I take it the small token of my appreciation arrived safely."

"They are absolutely breathtaking."

Sebastein was pleased that she liked the flowers. They talked on the phone for about fifteen minutes. She thanked Sebastein again for the flowers and they ended their conversation, reassuring each other that their plans for Charlene's party had not changed.

After the conversation, Alimar turned to Sebastein and asked, "What is she like, master?"

"She is as beautiful as the goddess of nature. Sometimes I see her smiling face above the Heaven of the seven seas, and I am sad when I awake, realizing it was only a dream. She has captured the insight of my mind and has restored the joy within my soul."

4

Later that evening, about 8:00 P.M., Sebastein was once again at the Ryans' home. Benjamin appeared a little more pleasant towards him. "Good evening, sir. Do come in."

"Would you be so kind as to tell Monique that I am here," said Sebastein.

"Very well, sir."

Sebastein watched Monique as she slowly walked down the stairs. He was pleased.

"You're truly a masterpiece of God's creation, for even the beauty of Helen of Troy cannot be compared. Indeed, the gods have not forsaken me, for it surely is a gift from them to behold such a sight."

Monique smiled, walked up to him, gently kissed him on the cheek and said, "For the flowers."

Sebastein blushed and hung his head. Benjamin saw the kiss, cleared his throat, and then slowly walked away like someone suffering from psychomotor retardation.

They walked hand in hand to Sebastein's car. "Nice car," she said, sliding into the passenger seat.

"Thank you."

During their conversation, Monique happened to glance at the speedometer. "Maybe we ought to slow down just a little," she said.

"Sorry, I didn't realize I was going so fast."

She smiled as she snuggled up close to him, resting her head on his shoulder as they both remained silent for the rest of the journey.

Soon they were pulling up to the Savoy estate, which had been in Charlene's family for three generations. They had to drive along a winding path since Charlene's cottage sat at the other end of the property, with a comfortable enough distance between it and the mansion. Charlene had a pool built next to the cottage because she loved pool parties. Mr. and Mrs. Savoy were the perfect match for each other because they were from stoic upbringing. They often wondered how they had given birth to such a wild spirit as Charlene.

Sebastein pulled up to an area near the cottage. It was the designated parking lot for the evening. There were at least ten cars already. Monique identified the cars by their owners for Sebastein and gave him a little blurb about each personality before they got out of the car. The noise coming from behind the cottage sent a clear signal that fun was in the making.

Monique took Sebastein by the hand and led him toward the front door to the cottage. The door opened upon a light push. Only the clatter of pots and pans in the kitchen could be heard; no one else was in the house. It was clear that Monique knew her way around quite well. She led Sebastein through a few hallways into the backyard, where the party was already in full swing.

Sebastein looked around and noticed that the entertainment ranged from dancers to a live calypso band. Monique saw Sebastein looking at one of the dancers doing the limbo.

"Would you like us to try it?" asked Monique

"I'm afraid my poor back couldn't take it," replied Sebastein with a slight laughter.

"Hi, Monique, I'll be right there," shouted Charlene as she shimmied under the limbo stick. Monique waved to her.

"She is actually quite good, isn't she?" commented Sebastein.

A few minutes later, Charlene greeted Monique with a kiss on the cheek as she shook Sebastein's hand.

"Glad you could come, Sebastein."

Before Sebastein could respond, Monique asked angrily, "What is he doing here?" They all stared at Paul across the pool.

"Paul? I invited him. Why?"

"Why? You know I can't stand him."

"You know he doesn't mean any harm. He is just a horny son of a bitch who has the hots for you," replied Charlene.

"He is a creep and I don't know why Dad keeps him around."

"Because he is a damn good attorney, that's why. Are you going to stand there and worry about Paul all night, or are you and Sebastein going to come and do the limbo with me?" asked Charlene as she pulled both of them over toward the calypso band. One by one the three of them took turns going under the limbo stick.

"Very good, Sebastein, but then again this type of thing is in your blood, isn't it?" asked Paul.

Sebastein simply shook his head and ignored Paul.

"Don't let him get to you, Sebastein," Charlene said.

"Is he always this friendly?" he asked.

After a few more songs, the music stopped in order for Charlene to make an announcement. "Listen, everybody, it's time to go skinny-dipping in the pool. Feel free to change in any of the rooms." Before she could finish her announcement many of her guests were already stripping by the poolside.

"Well, shall we join them?" asked Monique.

Sebastein was very surprised by her question. "No, no, I'll pass on this one. Besides I didn't bring bathing trunks."

Monique giggled. "I knew you were going to say that." She took him by the hand and led him to a room in Charlene's home. She picked up a gift-wrapped box and presented it to him. "Now you do. See you by the pool," Monique said as she went to change.

Sebastein opened the box, then shook his head in disbelief after seeing a brand new pair of swim trunks. A few minutes later Sebastein emerged from the house. His daily exercise routine had done him well because as he wandered around looking for Monique, heads turned to admire his athletic frame. His broad shoulders gave way to a firm stomach on which you could bounce a ball easily, and those slender thighs glistened as he made his stride around the pool.

"Over here, Sebastein," screamed Monique, who was already in the pool.

"Jump in, Sebastein," screamed Charlene on the other side of the pool.

Before Sebastein could jump in, he was pushed into the pool from behind. When he landed in the water, he continued to descend head first toward the bottom of the pool. Concerned that he might hit his head before being able to regain his equilibrium, several swimmers rushed over to where Sebastein had made his entrance into the water. Soon Sebastein's head surfaced and everyone breathed a sigh of relief.

"I hope you don't mind, Sebastein. I figured you needed an extra push," said Paul laughing.

Sebastein did not reply.

"Feel like racing, Sebastein?" Charlene asked.

"Sure," Sebastein replied.

The swimmers went to one end of the pool and raced to the other end. They did this several times; each time Monique and Charlene were the winners as Sebastein struggled just to reach the finishing line.

"Too much for your old bones, Sebastein?" asked Paul.

Sebastein looked at the 29-year-old, well-built man and replied, "Perhaps."

"How about a little race between the two of us? I'll even give you a head start," said Paul.

"Maybe some other time," said Sebastein.

"What's the matter, boy, are you afraid?"

Everyone suddenly became silent as they glued their eyes to Sebastein, watching and waiting to see how he would react. Sebastein looked over at Monique, who was quiet with a certain sad look on her face. "Oh well, just one little race, but only on condition that we start together, head to head," said Sebastein.

"Whatever you say boy," replied Paul as he turned and swam to the head of the pool.

Both men were now at the head of the pool, waiting to start. Sebastein looked at Monique and winked at her.

"Why don't we make this more interesting. How about a little wager?" Paul asked.

"What did you have in mind?"

"The keys to my Ferrari in exchange for the keys to your Lamborghini."

"Don't you think you are taking this thing just a little bit too far?"

"What's the matter, boy, are you afraid?"

Once again, the spectators became silent, waiting to see how Sebastein would respond. No one likes to be called "boy," and they all knew the derogatory meaning it carried when it was directed by a white person to a Black person. Meanwhile, Sebastein tried everything to restrain himself from punching Paul in the gut. At last he smiled at Paul and simply said, "Okay, you got yourself a bet, boy."

Charlene volunteered to start the race, "On your marks, get set . . ." As Charlene said "Go," Paul dived off the edge of the pool full speed ahead. Everyone watched as Sebastein remained as if frozen in his get-ready position.

"Jump, Sebastein," shouted Monique.

"Damn it, Sebastein, will you jump?" screamed another voice from the audience.

Sebastein stood on the edge of the pool in position but refused to jump into the water. By this time Paul was halfway along the length of the pool. Finally Sebastein jumped in. His body went all the way to the bottom, then like a dolphin entertaining an audience, he leapt from under the water as a mighty force pulled him through the air like a bird to the winning end of the pool.

Paul continued to struggle toward the end of the pool, not realizing that Sebastein was already ahead of him, sitting up on the edge. Paul lifted his head above the water, wiped his face, and looked behind him to see whether Sebastein was somewhere around. A big smile came on his face when he did not see Sebastein. But suddenly he noticed how the crowd was laughing and staring at him in the water and pointing. He looked around only to see Sebastein with a big grin on his face. Paul finally made it to the end of the pool, almost out of breath.

"What took you so long?" Sebastein asked.

Within minutes, Sebastein was surrounded by people. Basically everyone wanted to find out how he had done that, how is it possible to dive into the pool and emerge the way he did, such great distance, how is it possible for any man to do that? They were all curious, all amazed.

Sebastein smiled and said, "In my country it is called 'rituals of the dolphin.' Anyone can do it." Though in his mind he knew this was only an excuse. Nevertheless they believed him, for they had to believe that what they had seen had really happened.

As the crowd around Sebastein slowly dispersed, Monique looked at him, went over, and for the first time gave him a passionate kiss. Paul, looking on, felt the blood rushing through his veins.

Paul said, "I don't know what you did, Sebastein, how you got to this end so quickly, but you must have cheated."

Sebastein, without replying, looked at him and walked away with Monique by his side.

Still somewhat embarrassed, Paul screamed, "One last wager, Sebastein. That is, of course, if you are man enough."

Sebastein stopped, turned around and replied, "What did you have in mind this time?"

"Something you can't cheat on so easily. Let's go to the bottom of the pool. The first one to come up for air loses. The last one to come up for air is the winner. That way I can look at you and you can look at me, and no more tricks."

"Someone could get hurt doing that."

"What's the matter? Are you chicken?" asked Paul loudly, once again trying to entice Sebastein into another competitive endeavor.

"What type of wager did you have in mind this time?"

Paul quickly replied, "How about $50,000 to the winner?"

"Are you sure you want to do that?"

"If it is too steep for you, we can drop it down to about $100," Paul said, laughing while the people who were watching on laughed also.

Sebastein stared at them for a while and then said, "No, $50,000 is quite okay. Keep in mind, however, that you may be walking home tonight." The spectators laughed even louder once again.

Monique, with great concern, pulled Sebastein aside and asked him if he was crazy. "Don't worry, Monique. I have this covered."

"Take a good look around you, Sebastein. All these kids are rich, spoiled kids. Fifty thousand dollars is nothing to them. To Paul it is something he probably loses gambling everyday. It's nothing to these people. Are you sure you want to bet that much?"

Sebastein was a bit disappointed in her and stated softly, "And you think because I am a Black man I can't afford it, is that it?"

"I did not say that. But I just want you to think about what you are doing. You don't have anything to prove to me or to these people. You don't have anything to prove to Paul. So why are you doing it?"

"I am doing it to prove to you."

She was surprised at his answer and did not trouble him with her concerns anymore. She kissed him softly on the cheek and simply said, "Go get him, tiger," as people gathered around and watched both men slowly descend to the bottom of the pool. Paul and Sebastein sat at the bottom of the pool, face-to-face. Paul thought that this would be the easiest $50,000 he had ever won gambling. Both men looked up above them and saw their spectators looking down, anxiously awaiting the outcome of this game.

Sebastein folded his legs, closed his eyes, and sat at the bottom of the pool as if he was at ease with his environment. Paul also seemed very calm and relaxed, still wondering and hoping that Sebastein would emerge within a few minutes. But his hope and his wondering was in vain because Sebastein sat there with his eyes closed, reflecting on a time in another land when spending hours beneath the ocean was a daily routine for him and his people, to whom such an activity was as common as taking a swim in the pool. Sebastein's thoughts were interrupted a few minutes after by bubbling and thrashing in the water. He opened his eyes to see Paul, gasping for air, struggling to reach the top.

Paul made it to the top of the pool, gasping for breath. This was the longest he had stayed under water because this time he had a worthy opponent. Paul took a deep breath, shook his head, looked down and saw Sebastein still at the bottom of the pool with his eyes closed, as if he was sitting in a monastery in total reflection of his daily life. Seven minutes had passed and people started to look at one another, wondering whether or not Sebastein was alright.

Monique was very concerned and dived into the pool to rescue Sebastein. As she approached Sebastein, he opened his eyes and smiled. She signaled him to go up, but he shook his head, no. A frown came over her face because now she was baffled. He sat her down at the bottom of the pool, folded her legs under her, and signaled for her to close her eyes. He then held her hands and they both sat there for another seven minutes, holding hands. The onlookers began to wonder. They were very worried because they had never witnessed anything like that before.

Sebastein then got up, still holding Monique's hand as they both emerged at the water's surface together. As they stepped out of the pool people gathered around with towels, drying them off and asking, "How did he do that? How is it possible?"

"It is not humanly possible for anyone to stay under the water that long without getting air," said a male guest.

Sebastein looked at the gentleman who made that comment and said, "But you have witnessed that even Monique is able to do that."

"But how? I am a doctor and I know it is humanly impossible to do that."

"Doctor, we only use a small portion of our minds. But I am able to develop and use a larger portion of my mind, and to teach people how to expand the use of their minds. I have taught Monique by holding her hands and being one with her mind. It is humanly possible to do these things if people just allow themselves, free themselves from all troubles, from all negative forces and be one with their elements, whether it may be wind or rain."

The doctor was still puzzled, but knew that there had to be some validity to what he just heard because he himself was a witness to the entire episode.

"Monique, did you know you were under the water for at least seven minutes, if not a little bit longer? How did you do it?" asked Charlene.

"Well, I wasn't aware of it. My eyes were closed, then I had this strange feeling. I felt very, very comfortable. I knew I had air. I wasn't breathing, but I knew my body was getting air. It's a feeling I have never had before."

Sebastein said, "It's a feeling that comes from within."

Paul came over to congratulate Sebastein on his victory. "You are quite a fish, Sebastein."

"Thank you," replied Sebastein.

"I will have the money first thing in the morning."

"What? Don't you carry that much cash around with you? I don't want your money or your car."

"You don't want $50,000? That's a whole lot of money for somebody like you."

"I already have a great deal of money. But you can do us both a favor by keeping the hell away from me."

Sebastein then took Monique by the hand and walked with her along the poolside, trying to get away from the crowd. He then whispered, "Would you mind very much if we leave now?"

Monique replied, "I think that's a great idea."

They both went inside to change and a few minutes later they were outside thanking Charlene for the wonderful time they had and bidding her farewell.

"I'll call you tomorrow," said Charlene.

Monique kissed her on the cheek and said, "Okay, I'll talk to you tomorrow."

Charlene looked at Sebastein and shook her head. "Mr. Sebastein, you are an amazing fellow."

Sebastein said, "Thank you, and thank you for having me at your party," as he and Monique headed to the car.

5

Sebastein's car cruised along the few miles that separated the Savoy and Ryan estates. One side of the road traced the waters of the Atlantic Ocean, where the incoming tide gave way to a swishing sound as the water washed the rocks in its path. Rolling hills bedecked with mansions bordered the other side of the road. The homes were a sight to behold, but at 2:00 A.M. only the lights from the houses beamed. There was light traffic on the road, each vehicle taking its own time as if marching to the beat of its own drum. Monique and Sebastein were engrossed in their own thoughts about the events of the evening.

Marvin Gaye started crooning "Let's Get It On" from the cassette Sebastein had slipped into the stereo soon after he got into the car. They had listened to the tail end of "Sexual Healing." Monique moved her head slowly to the beat of the song; it was one of her longtime favorites, and besides, she just loved Marvin's sexy voice. Strangely enough, before meeting Sebastein, she did not think much of Black people, but had always liked their songs and admired their athletic abilities. Suddenly, she felt devilish. She turned to Sebastein and said, "Let's go to your place."

"Are you sure you want to do that?" Sebastein asked, a bit surprised at her request.

She moved over closer to Sebastein until her head was gently resting on his shoulders. Her skin was so soft against his bare arm. He could smell her perfume, which was now tinged with the smell of chlorine from the pool. He tried to keep his eyes on the road but could not suppress the feelings that were beginning to well up inside him. Monique raised her head slightly, looked at Sebastein and said softly, "I'm sure."

Tires started screeching and the smell of rubber was everywhere as Sebastein made a U-turn and headed toward his home. Although he was delighted that she wanted to be with him, all that would have to wait for at least another hour before they would get to his home. But Sebastein had his collections of oldies but goodies to keep the tempo. If Smokey, Manilow, and Whitney couldn't do it, then no one could.

At 3:30 A.M. they were finally pulling up to a twelve-foot-high iron gate. As the car came within two feet of the gate, it started to open as Sebastein pressed a button that was installed in the dashboard.

"Oh, that's really neat!" said Monique. She then turned to look out the car window, trying to get a peek at the grounds. The car was going up a slight incline and she could see a structure dimly lit at the top. The final bend in the road revealed a structure of the most exquisite style. Nestled against the trees was a mansion, painted all white on the exterior. The mansion's magnificent look was made even more impressive by the intricately landscaped yard that encircled the building like a flowing skirt.

Monique was impressed. "Is this your home?"

"Yes."

"I thought we lived in a mansion. This place is about twice as large as ours. How many rooms are there?"

"Twenty-four bedrooms."

"Twenty-four? I feel sorry for your maid!" Monique responded with a chuckle.

Sebastein smiled and turned off the ignition as they were now stopped in front of the house. Before they could get out of the car, the front door to Sebastein's home opened and three men, dressed in their Egyptian attire, walked toward the car. One of the men extended his hand to assist Monique as she was getting out of the car. Before Monique could say thanks, all three men got down on their knees as if in reverence to her and kissed her feet. The men slowly rose from their knees; one went to park the car while the other two walked slowly behind Monique and Sebastein as they entered the mansion.

"They do that to all your guests?" Monique whispered.

"No, they don't."

"Then why me?"

"Maybe it is because they sense that you are a very special person to me."

By now they had passed through the foyer and through double doors into a circular living room. The room was handsomely decorated, with each piece of furniture appearing to have been specially selected, having its own meaning and purpose in the decorator's plan. There were artifacts reflecting Sebastein's travels around the globe. But it was the walls that held the true treasures. Like a collage, the walls were adorned with original paintings from the masters, segmented to reveal stories from different eras. Monique stood in the middle of the floor, transfixed to Jacques-Louis David's painting of Socrates lying in bed, surrounded by his friends, after he had swallowed the hemlock. She had admired the great philosopher ever since reading about him during a humanities course in college.

Sebastein walked up behind Monique and with his arms around her waist, he said "Aren't you sleepy yet?"

"I am, but this room. Oh, it's a treasure!"

"Trust me, you will have more than enough time to study each piece. But it's time you had some rest. We've both had a long day and night."

Sebastein escorted Monique from the living room to the staircase that led to the upper level on the east wing of the house. This was where the bedrooms were. Sebastein's room was on this side of the house because he preferred to rise with the sun. He opened the door to one of the bedrooms and said, "You can use this one." He showed her where things were kept, and she admired him because for a man of his stature the intricacies of where things are in guest rooms were usually relegated to housekeepers.

"Where is your room?" she asked.

"Mine is right next to yours." He kissed her on the forehead and said, "Sleep tight, and if you need anything just press that button above your bed."

"What will happen? Would you come?"

"Maybe, or if not me Alimar will surely come."

"Who is Alimar?"

"The most elderly of the servants who kissed your feet."

"Oh, I see. I will be sure to remember his name. I don't have many men kissing my feet."

"That's hard to believe." He kissed her once again and said goodnight.

It was 4:30 by the time Monique hit the bed. She was tired, and would have fallen asleep in minutes had she been in her own bed. She didn't know if it was the strange surroundings, but she couldn't go to sleep right away. She kept tossing and turning. Frankly, when she had suggested coming home with Sebastein she hadn't planned on being alone. Fine time for him to be the gentleman.

In the other room, Sebastein also lay restless. He wanted to be with Monique but didn't want to give her the impression that she had to because she was in his home. Monique looked at the button above her head and contemplated whether or not she should press it. With her mind fully made up, she attempted to press the button but was interrupted by a knock at the door. She opened the door and saw Sebastein.

He looked at her and asked, "Is everything alright?"

She stared at him for a moment and then said, "Yes."

"Okay then, good-night," and he turned and walked off.

Before Sebastein could enter his room, there was a loud roar of thunder and Monique screamed. He rushed to her and held her closely in his arms. She was shaking. They listened together as the thunder continued to roll. Suddenly, it began to rain. As the rain beat harder and harder against the window, they found themselves engrossed in each other's arms. Their lips found each other and lingered passionately, as Sebastein felt a little guilty for messing with Mother Nature to ensure his own sexual gratification.

They removed each other's clothing slowly, and Sebastein found himself caressing her with his tongue, from her neck down to her legs, as she moaned, closing her eyes and enjoying his tongue as it finally found a soft and tender spot between her legs. Her moaning became louder as she pressed his head, trying to get his tongue inside of her as far as possible. As Sebastein continued to take her, she moved like a sparrow in heat, making unusual sounds contrary to the species of rarity. As he continued to probe the main source of her suppressed emotions, her vision of clearness became blurred by the tears of delight. He raised his head and kissed her lips passionately, as she clenched him tightly between her breasts with fingers like thorns in the midst of his back. He penetrated her and it calmed the hotness of her blood, yet her body continued to move in convulsions like a fire within the ocean. They indulged in the agony of pleasure, fumbled in excitement as they investigated and explored various regions of their bodies. Like a nemesis, Sebastein continued to heighten her sexual thirst, giving her the benefit of his unlimited experience. Tears rushed down her face, as the perspiration of her body became the melting pot of lubrication that showered from a tormented organ.

She was breathless with a plea of mercy in her eyes and a sense of hesitation was in the air. Sebastein continued to spread her legs apart as an open universe collided, causing her lower body to move like a planet on its axis, hungering for a need to fill a cavity, to create an explosion and a rage of ecstasy. A final scream by both lovers signified they had reached and touched the face of the Empyrean.

Meanwhile, Sebastein's servants gathered downstairs in the basement, performing a ritual that symbolizes the renaissance of a new love and a prolonged soul. Alimar, the leader of this ritual, told the other servants, who were still on their knees, "It is done. Our master lives." Sebastein and Monique had fallen asleep, cuddled in each other's arms.

Monique was awakened by the dazzling of the sun beaming into the room. She realized that Sebastein was no longer in the bed with her. The rain had stopped and it appeared that a bright and sunny day was in the making. Monique got up and slipped into Sebastein's robe, which was hanging on the bathroom door. She couldn't remember seeing it there when she had washed up for bed earlier that morning. She wandered around the east wing for a few minutes, then headed downstairs to see the remainder of the beautiful place. On her way downstairs she noticed the servants bustling about as they attended to their morning chores.

On seeing her, one of the servants said, "It is the chosen one." Immediately they all rushed to the foot of the stairs and knelt in respect to a woman who was as much a stranger to them as they were to her. Monique found the servants' actions quite curious, but she continued to make her descent. She was particularly bewildered by what the servant said about her being the "chosen one." As Monique got closer to the servants she said, "Please do not kneel to me."

The servants got up, yet their heads were still hung as if they were either ashamed or dared not look at her.

"May we continue with our duties, madam?" Alimar asked.

Although she was surprised by the question she said, "Sure, please, by all means. Go right ahead."

As the servants went on their way, she called to the one who had made the request on behalf of his colleagues and asked, "Are you Alimar?"

"Yes, madam, I am."

She looked at Alimar and asked, "What did he mean when he said I was the chosen one?"

Alimar was lost for words. He didn't know how to answer the question.

Almost on cue, a voice came from the top of the stairs. "That will be all, Alimar."

Monique looked up the stairs and saw Sebastein.

He said to her jokingly, "I see you are an early bird."

Disregarding what was troubling her moments earlier, Monique ran up the stairs toward Sebastein, hugging him around the waist as they slowly went back to the room together.

"I was wondering where you were," said Monique.

They lay on the bed quietly, staring at each other as they caressed each other's faces. Sebastein studied the contours of her face. Her eyes were olive green, contrasted against the auburn tint of her hair. They were growing fond of each other.

"Where are you from, Sebastein?"

"What do you mean?"

"Well, I detect a slight accent. I can't figure it out. Where were you born?"

Sebastein turned over on his back with both hands beneath his head and softly repeated the question. "Where was I born? That's a good question."

"Well?" said Monique as she tickled him under the arms.

"I am from a land where peace has never been and war prevails. A land where the lights are bright and the drums beat to the sound of lovers' hearts. I am from a land where iniquity and darkness were once the essence of life, a land where the crucifixion of my people has often angered the supreme being. Yet they fail to do anything to rectify the situation because they have become immune to such sacrifices. I am from a land where children play in harmony and the wildest of beasts is as tame as a dove, a land where I have seen light within darkness and heaven within hell as mankind perceives them to be. A land where empires come crumbling down due to the corruption that roars in their midst. A land where the women are so beautiful and bewitching to men that even in the times of death they welcome it with open arms. I am from a land where people are afraid to judge you for who you are for fear they might find out that you are just like them."

As Sebastein continued to talk, Monique noticed that his words brought tears to his eyes. "Yes, I am from a land where the cry of my people has gone unnoticed, a land where pain and suffering have become sports of the gods. And because we have seen all these things and have tried to change them, we were cast aside like the tides of the ocean."

Monique interrupted him, "We? What do you mean by we?"

Realizing that it was a slip of the tongue, Sebastein decided to play it off. "Oh, I am sorry. Did I say we? I meant me of course."

Monique gently wiped the tears from his eyes with her hands and he leaned over and kissed her. Although she did not get the answer she was looking for, she could sense that it was a painful topic and decided not to pursue it further.

Their togetherness was interrupted by a buzz from the intercom. It was Alimar telling them that breakfast would be served within a few minutes. They got up and went to the bathroom to take a shower together. In the shower, they caressed each other's bodies as they took turns with the soap. This interlude was enough to satisfy their libidos until perhaps later.

The dining room boasted an antique table twenty feet long. Monique was seated at one end of the table and Sebastein at the other. They ate in silence for a while, glancing at each other between bites and swallows. Sebastein's thoughts were interrupted by Alimar, who whispered something in his ear. After Alimar departed, Sebastein closed his eyes for a few seconds.

Monique became very concerned as she asked, "Is everything alright, Sebastein?" Still in deep thought and with his eyes closed, Sebastein did not hear Monique's question. "Is everything okay, Sebastein?" she repeated a little louder.

Sebastein's eyes slowly opened. "You have a visitor," he said.

"A visitor? Me? Here?"

Sebastein described the person to Monique. It did not take much description before she realized who it was.

"That's Nick. He must have followed us here."

"Who is Nick?"

"My bodyguard."

"Your bodyguard!"

"Yes. My father thought I needed one after what happened to me on the beach."

"Oh, I see. Is he the same fellow who was hiding in the bushes?"

"That's him alright."

"Well, should we invite him to breakfast?"

"Of course not. He's on the job so let him stay on the job."

They both smiled and paid no more attention to the incident.

After breakfast, Sebastein took Monique on a tour of his estate and later on they both went horseback riding. During one of their fateful ventures on the horses, Monique was several feet ahead of Sebastein, riding with full speed ahead as Sebastein deliberately allowed her to indulge in her victory. Suddenly the horse threw her in the air.

Sebastein reacted instantaneously, bringing his horse to a complete stop. He stared in the direction in which Monique was about to fall on her head, and rather than coming down on her head she was now slowly being brought down gently on her buttocks by some force. Monique was a little bit shocked at being thrown by the horse, but was more than curious about what happened after. She looked to Sebastein for answers but he ignored the episode and focused more on consoling her, making sure she was alright.

Seconds later, Monique got up to examine the horse. She noticed that his right front leg was broken. She had a soft spot for horses, having been around them since she was a toddler.

Gallant Knight became her horse to own when she was six years old. She had watched his birth through a hole in the stable, and served as surrogate mother to the baby horse, whose mother died during childbirth. She and Gallant Knight were like bosom buddies for the next ten years until he died a mysterious death one evening. The horse Sebastein gave her to ride brought back those mixed memories.

Monique kissed the horse on its forehead. She knew that its leg was broken because she had seen that dozens of times before. "Don't worry," she whispered in its ears, "we'll get help for you."

"Let me take a look at the leg. I'm sure it's just a sprain." Sebastein stooped down, turned his back to block Monique's view, and with both hands on the broken leg he uttered to himself, "You are alright now, boy. Everything is just fine." As he got up, he said to Monique, "See, it was just a little sprain," and led the horse around in a circle. Monique noticed that strangely enough the horse seemed to have recovered fully. She was very happy that neither she nor the horse had suffered a much worse fate.

Soon thereafter, they mounted the horses, but this time they rode at a leisurely stride. After another twenty minutes, they stopped to rest for a while under a tree. As they sat down, Monique got close to Sebastein and put her head in his lap. Sebastein gazed into her eyes while he ran his fingers through her hair.

With emotions in his heart, Sebastein said to her,

"How deep my feelings lie in my heart for thee.
Behold your love has filled my mood with joy
And given life to the offspring of my spirit.
I welcome thee within my heart,
O flaming star of my eyes.
I will worship the ground thou walkest on
And give praise to the one
Who created such beauty which I behold.
I will sing and rejoice,
Pledging to loyalty and trust in our love,
Binding our vow with the kiss of seal.
Truly, truly my love is sincere;
My eyes shed the tears of love
While my body trembles from fear.
Heavens forbid if my love is unreal;
May I also die before I break the kiss of seal."

"I didn't know you liked poetry."
"Yes, I do."
"Recite another."
He looked at her once again as the words flowed softly off his tongue.

"Truly, truly you proclaim me a friend,
For the things we do are indeed the things of a friend.

Yet there are times when I wish,
I wish we could advance beyond such a stage.
For to know you, one could also learn to love you.
I am nothing more than what you see,
But in the presence of your company
I am thrilled for you honor me.
You have captured the insight of my mind
And restored the joy within my soul.
You have complemented my every desire in a mate.
Yet I share my feelings reluctantly
For I fear that in your eyes I can only be a friend.
Yes, this is only a wish, a wish to go a stage beyond."

Sebastein's words sent a chill up Monique's spine and she kissed him passionately, for she knew that in that poem was a message that even the deaf could hear. Her kiss was an acknowledgement to his request. They sat there and talked for a while, taking the time to learn about each other, loving, caressing, and gleaming at each other as if they were the only two souls in the world.

Realizing that it was almost past lunch time, the two headed back to Sebastein's mansion. When they reached the stables, they left the horses in the care of the stable hands.

As they walked back to the house, Monique said, "I guess it is time for me to leave."

"Please stay a little longer. Perhaps I could interest you in some shopping in Beverly Hills? You can have anything you want on Rodeo Drive. I really would like to spend some more time with you."

The sound of the word "shopping" was a delight to Monique's ears. Clothes were her weakness. She shopped for fun, on special occasions, and when she was feeling down. She would invent an excuse to shop. "I can stay a bit longer. Besides, I haven't been to Beverly Hills in a few months and I am sure the shops are featuring the upcoming fall line. I can't think of a better way to spend the afternoon."

"Then it's all settled."

"I almost forgot about Nick. I am sure he's still outside waiting patiently in his car for me to come out."

"For that dedication, I sincerely hope your father is paying him quite well," Sebastein said as he tried to restrain a laugh. They hugged each other as they walked into the house.

"Are we having lunch inside today?" Sebastein asked Alimar.

"No, master. Lunch is already set in the cabana."

"Very well," Sebastein said as he turned Monique around and headed back outside to the other side of the house. As expected, a sumptuous lunch was set for two, with a bottle of wine being chilled in a nearby pitcher. Two servants, dressed in white, waited for their commands, but Sebastein dismissed them because he wanted to be alone with Monique.

During lunch, they shared regrets and childhood experiences. At one point Monique wanted to ask him what he did for a living, but remembering his answer at Charlene's party, she decided not to press the issue, at least not for the moment. Still, she was curious how someone so young could have acquired so much wealth at a time when such wealth is seldom even displayed by the elite, regardless of their race. Although Sebastein knew her hidden thoughts, when he felt the need to probe he did not make her aware that such was the case.

Later that day, Sebastein fulfilled his promise and took Monique shopping. They went by way of helicopter so that Monique would have ample time and not have to rush through the shops or be inconvenienced by traffic. Sebastein treated Monique to more things than she had imagined.

By 7:00 P.M. they were back at Sebastein's mansion. Monique insisted on taking Sebastein to dinner that evening. Sebastein informed his servants that they were dining out that evening. He told them they should take the rest of the evening off, a kind of generosity that was displayed quite frequently by the person they called their master.

6

It was now 8:00 P.M. Monique and Sebastein were dressed and on their way out to have dinner. Monique was wearing a full-length, off-the-shoulder lace dress with a slit in the front all the way up to her mid-thigh. Her hair was pulled to the top of her head in a French roll. A diamond necklace and matching earrings completed the outfit. She had picked these up on her shopping spree earlier. Sebastein wore a black tuxedo.

As they drove off the estate, Sebastein noticed that a car was behind them. He knew it was Monique's bodyguard. Sebastein turned to her and asked, "Would you mind very much if just for tonight I lose our friend?"

Monique looked behind and saw that it was Nick following her. The first day Nick was assigned to protect her, she had thought it was kind of cute. But his round-the-clock surveillance was becoming a drag. She felt he was invading her privacy because he would appear at the most inopportune moments. Monique looked at Sebastein and said, "By all means, Bond, let's lose him."

At the sound of those words, Sebastein stepped on the accelerator and within seconds the speedometer had climbed to one hundred miles per hour. As they approached a bend, Monique closed her eyes and held her breath. She hadn't planned on dying in a car crash and certainly not tonight. After all, she was just getting to know this man, who seemed a bit strange in a cute sort of way.

They made it around the corner and Monique breathed a sigh of relief. "My God, you do drive like Bond," she said with a serious look on her face.

Sebastein did not reply. His focus was on the road as he continued to guide the speeding Lamborghini around traffic and narrow pathways, just like Agent 007 in the James Bond series. A few minutes later Nick's car was nowhere in sight and Sebastein knew that he had lost him. Before Sebastein could reduce speed he heard sirens behind him. He checked his rearview mirror and realized that it was the cops. He pulled over, looked at Monique and said, "You win some, you lose some."

Monique and Sebastein sat in the car quietly as they waited for the officers. Two Caucasian officers came up to Sebastein's car, one on either side. They shined their flashlights into the car and were surprised to see Sebastein and Monique together.

"Roll down the window and give me your driver's license, boy," said one of the officers to Sebastein.

Sebastein rolled down the window slowly, and handed his license and registration to the cop. The officer looked at the photograph on the license, then at Sebastein, then he walked toward his car. The other officer stayed on the passenger's side of Sebastein's car with the flashlight still shining in Monique's face.

A few minutes later the officer came back from the patrol car. "Step out of the car with your hands where I can see them. No funny moves now or you're dead meat."

"What seems to be the problem, officer?" Sebastein asked.

The officer became annoyed and shouted angrily, "Get out of the car, nigger!"

"You too, nigger lover," said the other officer to Monique.

They both followed the officers' instructions and got out of the car.

"Say, Charlie, I think this boy is drunk," said Gus, the officer who was standing beside Sebastein to the other officer who was with Monique. He looked at Sebastein and asked, "Are you drunk, boy?" Sebastein was quiet.

"Where does a nigger get the money to buy a car like this?" Charlie asked. Sebastein again remained quiet.

"Got to be drugs!" shouted Gus. He looked at Sebastein and asked, "Are you dealing drugs, boy?"

Sebastein remained silent. He was playing it cool because he knew that even in this day and age, there were white men who couldn't stand to see a Black man with a white woman. He knew that Charlie and Gus were fishing for any reason to try to hurt him.

Meanwhile, Charlie looked at Monique from head to toe and back again. A grin came on his face and he said to her, "So, are you carrying any concealed weapon?" Monique didn't respond.

Charlie placed the flashlight on the top of the car and with both hands he started to frisk Monique slowly. He held her by the waist and made his way toward her behind, rubbing and squeezing. His hand made its way up the slit in her dress, then between her legs as he held her vagina, caressing it, and with his other hand he fumbled all over her breasts.

Monique was angry but remained silent, hoping that by doing so she would not bring any harm to Sebastein and herself. Tears of rage dripped down her face as the officer fumbled her vagina while his colleague kept Sebastein preoccupied. She felt his finger inside of her as she stood still and watched him indulging in his moment of glory with a smirk on his face. For the second time in her life she felt helpless, powerless, and violated, as if she was having a nightmare or one of those dreams where one is in danger, tries to scream for help, but no words seem to come. She bit on her lips as she covered her mouth with one hand, trying not to be overcome by the pain that rushed through her body as Charlie plucked a handful of hair from her vagina.

"I'll keep this for a souvenir," Charlie said as he put the handful of hair to his nose, sniffed it, then placed some in his mouth and chewed it sensuously before swallowing it.

By this time Gus was becoming more and more annoyed with Sebastein. "What's the matter, boy? Cat got your tongue?"

Sebastein stared at him then said, "Sometimes it is better to fight words with silence and defeat trouble with words, especially when a fool cannot help being a fool, just like a dog cannot be held responsible for his bad manners."

"Are you calling me a dog, nigger?"

"Whatever a man thinks in his heart and mind, so he is."

They were interrupted by bright lights from another oncoming patrol car. Sensing a sigh of relief from Sebastein, Gus waved at his buddies as one of them pushed his head out the window and shouted, "See you got a live one there. You boys seem to have everything under control. So I'll see you guys back at the precinct." The car passed without stopping.

Gus shouted over to Charlie, "That's Corey. Hell, he hates niggers as much as I do, especially the ones who think they're good enough to be going out with our women."

"Ain't that a bitch!" Charlie replied.

Turning back to Sebastein, Gus said, "You and your fine clothes and your fancy car, you look like a dressed up monkey. Are you a monkey, boy?" By this time his nose was touching Sebastein like a drill sergeant whipping a private into shape for Uncle Sam.

"Better to be a dressed up monkey than a candidate for Listerine."

Using his index finger, Gus tapped Sebastein on the lip, "Watch your mouth, you smart ass."

"Car 153, respond, car 153," interrupted a dispatcher on the radio. Gus and Charlie ran over to the patrol car. Monique and Sebastein looked at each other. Sebastein could see that she was terrified. He tried to comfort her with his eyes, as they both stood in the same spot where the officers had left them.

The officers returned to Sebastein's car. "You're one lucky nigger tonight. With more time I know I could break you and give me a reason to whip your ass. Next time," Gus said to Sebastein. Gus stretched out his hand to give Sebastein the license and registration, but deliberately let them fall before Sebastein had a grasp. With movements like lightning, Sebastein caught the documents before they hit the ground.

Gus was stunned at Sebastein's speed. He looked at Sebastein in a very strange way and remarked, "Goddamn, you niggers are fast."

Meanwhile, Charlie, devouring Monique with his eyes, leaned over and whispered in her ears, "Well, I think you are clean, ma'am. No concealed weapons, no drugs."

Both officers rushed back to their vehicle and went away without writing Sebastein a ticket. Although somewhat distraught by the entire event, the couple got back in the car and continued on their journey to what was intended to be a very pleasurable and enjoyable evening.

About half a mile down the road, Sebastein noticed that Monique was unusually quiet. He glanced at her for a while and said, "Some things will never change."

Monique did not respond and he noticed that rather than look at him she was looking outside the window. A perturbed look came over his face and suddenly he jammed on the brakes, sending his passenger rocketing in her seat like an astronaut taking off in a spaceship to the moon. He penetrated her mind and knew the burden she had borne during the entire episode by the so-called representatives of the law.

"You are stopping?" she asked.

"Why didn't you tell me?"

"Tell you what?" Monique asked.

He stared at her without another word and by looking at him somehow she realized that he knew what had happened. And she said softly, "Because I did not want them to hurt you."

The car came to a stop. Sebastein opened the door and got out.

"Where are you going?" Monique asked.

He looked at her and said in a very sharp tone of voice, "Stay in the car and don't come out."

The demanding tone in his voice allowed her to see for the first time another part of Sebastein that she had never seen before. She sat where she was and watched him as he walked around the car and stood a few feet away from her.

Monique watched Sebastein through the car window as a mysterious stranger from the past unleashed a telekinetic power, which is symptomatic of a generation of gods that once ruled the universe. And as she watched him standing there in a meditative state, she noticed a drastic change in the environment. It was like a hurricane was on its way. But there was no notice of this on the weather reports that day, and this was surely uncharacteristic for a summer night. The trees were shaking uncontrollably, as if they would lose their leaves in minutes. The strength of the wind was so strong that at times it shook the car. The clouds moved rapidly across the sky as thunder roared continuously and unusually loud.

Meanwhile, a few miles away, Gus and Charlie noticed the sudden change in the weather. "Charlie, boy I think we are witnessing the making of a storm," Gus said.

"Sure looks like it. Let's take this last call and get back to the station," Charlie suggested.

Gus agreed. As they continued to drive, they noticed that the lightning was getting closer and closer to the car. "I don't like the look of this," said Charlie.

"Don't worry, Charlie. I have never seen lightning hit anyone inside his car before."

Before he could finish his statement, a bolt of lightning came crashing through the windshield, striking Charlie in the chest. Gus looked over and saw that Charlie's chest was on fire. He tried to put out the fire but noticed that the car was speeding up and going faster and his brakes were not working. He kept jamming on the brakes, trying to stop the car, which was going close to a hundred miles per hour by now. He noticed a corner down the road and knew it was impossible to make that turn at the speed he was going. He started to panic as he tried harder and harder to stop the car, but it was impossible, for the car was in the hands of a man who stood miles away, a man who was filled with anger and pain and whose concept of mercy was consumed momentarily by the thought that he had stood there unaware while Monique was violated in every sense of the word.

Gus wrestled with the car in a futile effort to save his life. A glimpse of hope shed light on the futility of his effort as the car stopped suddenly at the edge of a steep cliff. A smirk of conquest overshadowed his face once again as he saw that even though the two front wheels of the car were hanging over the cliff, leaving the car at a standstill, he had been successful in bringing it to a halt, or so he thought. He tried to get out of the car but it tilted forward as if it was getting ready to take a head dive down the cliff. He stopped his movements in hopes that it would bring the car to a standstill once again, and it did.

Seconds later, an entity in the appearance of Sebastein presented itself in front of the windshield. The magnitude of Sebastein's image blocked Gus's view as he wiped his eyes in astonishment, thinking they were deceiving him. "What the . . ."

The voice of Sebastein interrupted. "Remember to explain your behavior to Mary should you enter our father's kingdom."

The end of Sebastein's words initiated the fading of his image and triggered a powerful wind that aided in sealing the officer's fate. His car went crashing down the cliff as a terrifying scream echoed across the mountainside.

Sebastein opened his eyes because he knew the outcome. Then he uttered to himself before getting back to Monique, "I fail to understand why people trouble trouble when trouble seldom troubles them." Sebastein slowly walked back to the car.

Monique noticed the sudden change in the atmosphere once again. This time there was no turbulence, no hurricane symptoms, rather total calmness as if it was once again heeding to the command of entities beyond the heavens. She continued to watch Sebastein as he got back into the car and hung his head over the steering wheel. Monique moved closer to him and gently raised his cheek from off the steering wheel and for the second time she saw tears in his eyes. Then she leaned over closer and kissed him, and without any more words, they sat there in each other's arms for another half an hour.

"Would you rather if we just return home?" asked Monique.

"No, Besides, it is not every day that such a beautiful young lady as yourself invites me out to dinner, and I don't know when I'll ever get the chance again."

Monique smiled and responded, "I guess you are right. Why should we let those jerks ruin our evening?"

"So young and so innocent, yet so wise." Sebastein said to her with a gleam in his eyes.

"I am not as innocent as you think. And as far as my age, I am old enough to do whatever you want me to do, and young enough to learn whatever you want to teach me," she said with a smile.

"I'll remember that," replied Sebastein as they drove off toward their destination.

7

It was 9:30 P.M. by the time Monique and Sebastein pulled up in front of Les Champs, Monique's favorite restaurant. Their reservation was for 9:00. They had called ahead from the car phone and the maître d' assured them that he would hold the reservation. As soon as they got out of the car, an attendant jumped in to take it to the garage.

"Mademoiselle Ryan, so good to see you again," beamed the maître d' at Monique. The Ryans were valued customers at Les Champs. They had patronized it for years. Monique had celebrated many special events here, such as making the dean's list her first semester in college.

"Bon soir, Henri. I would like you to meet my friend Sebastein."

"Enchanté, monsieur," replied Henri as he escorted the couple to their table tucked away at a secluded corner of the restaurant, overlooking the water. As they walked to the table, heads turned, some in admiration, some in envy, and others in disapproval. Henri pulled out the chair for Monique. He then turned to the two and said, "Bon appetite," as he sauntered away.

A complimentary bottle of Dom Perignon was sent over to their table, followed within minutes by their waiter, Pierre. Monique tried to place her order but Pierre lapsed into pure French. Monique was becoming a bit impatient because she was not getting through to Pierre, who had only arrived in the United States from his homeland, France, less than a month before. Sebastein stretched across the table and touched Monique's left hand, which was resting on the table as she struggled with bits and pieces of French she had picked up from a college course and a few trips abroad.

"Please, allow me," interrupted Sebastein.

Monique was surprised when Sebastein conversed in fluent French with Pierre. It was apparent that Sebastein was at ease with the language and its subtleties as he ordered for himself and Monique. She breathed a sigh of relief, recalling once she and Charlene, absolutely famished, popped in for a bite and the only waiter available spoke virtually no English. They ordered by pointing to the same item on the menu, and poked fun at each other when the waiter returned with ice cream floats. They simply pretended that all they had wanted was dessert, and ate to their hearts' content.

After Pierre left with their orders, Monique turned to Sebastein and said, "I didn't know you spoke French."

"Among other languages," Sebastein replied.

"How many languages do you speak?"

"A few."

Monique frowned in disbelief.

"Why do you find that so hard to believe?" Sebastein asked.

"Well, I don't know. Maybe because I have a problem learning any other language besides English."

Sebastein stared at the glass of Dom Perignon in his hand and uttered beneath his breath, "If you had lived as long as I have, seen the things that I have, and travelled the paths that I have, then you would know that there is no miracle in speaking the languages that I speak."

"You know, Sebastein, you act like a 39-year-old but sound like 150. What other languages do you speak besides French and English?"

"Arabic, German, Swahili, Chinese, and Russian."

"Russian? You speak Russian?"

"Yes, why does that surprise you?"

"I don't know. You are not a communist or anything like that, are you?" she asked jokingly.

"Who knows, maybe I am a KGB agent." They laughed as Sebastein reached across the table, took her hand, and began caressing it.

Sebastein's expression returned to seriousness as he stared piercingly at Monique, studying her face and the unpretentious sensuality she evoked. He raised both her hands to his lips and lightly brushed them with a kiss. As he returned her hands to the center of the table he started another of his poems, which he was becoming famous for with Monique.

"Behold, I see not only the heavenly image in which you
    appear,
For the sound of your voice reveals the inner beauty that lies
    within.
Doubt me not because your smile bears testimony to the truth.
Your beauty consumes the light in every man's eyes,
And your love is like a flower inside their hearts forever.
Open your heart, my beloved one, and examine my words.
For as the birds fly in the clouds not knowing what lies beyond,
So is it with one who sees the signs of love and is unable to
    recognize his identity.
Give rise to the thoughts
Suppress not thy feelings
Doubt me not
For the things I say need no justification.
For the way you are bears testimony to the truth."

When Sebastein was through, he leaned over and kissed her gently on the lips and whispered, "I love you, Monique."

"Pardon, monsieur et mademoiselle," interrupted Pierre before Monique could respond to Sebastein. Pierre had rolled up a cart to the couple's table and lifted the silver lids from the servers as the aroma from the dishes escaped into the air. Monique was please with the assortment of dishes, each a work of art. Pierre made a quick exit after he served the meals.

"I would like to make a toast in celebration of this occasion," said Monique. "Here's to us. To our friendship and to our love and may it continue to blossom until it blooms into something more precious than gold."

Sebastein was caught off guard for a few seconds, then he asked, "Do you love me?"

"Though strange as it may seem, especially since I don't know you very well, I know I do."

They leaned forward and kissed. Soon thereafter, Sebastein's mind wandered off to a table several feet from him. He turned his head slowly, gazing at a young man who seemed in his late twenties bound to a specialized wheelchair. The young man was paralyzed from his neck down. His head was positioned in a special device that allowed him to start a voice communicator merely by uttering a few simple passwords. His facial paralysis prevented him from communicating to his dinner companions that he needed help. The young man tried in vain to reach out to his guardians with his eyes but they were too consumed with their own pleasure to notice his discomfort.

Sebastein saw the discomfort on the young man's face; his lips were so dry that the skin was peeling from them. His functional enuresis caused the bag at his side to fill with wasted secretion. And to make matters worse, he was now at the point where his encopresis brought him to the need to defecate.

Monique noticed that Sebastein seemed miles away. "What's wrong, Sebastein?"

"It's the young man in the wheelchair."

"What about him?"

"Something is wrong."

"What? He seems fine and I am sure someone at the table would have noticed if he were in any trouble."

"Are you kidding? Look at them!" Sebastein got up from his chair.

"What are you going to do?"

"I'll be right back."

"Maybe you shouldn't interfere."

"There is a difference between interfering and assisting," replied Sebastein as he walked toward the young man in the wheelchair.

From the other side of the room, the maître d's eyes followed Sebastein as he made his way toward the paraplegic. A lady dining close by flipped open a pocket mirror, pretending to check her lipstick, while all the time watching Sebastein's strides. "Is your food alright, dear?" asked the gentleman seated with her, looking as if he was eating for all the hungry kids in Rwanda. "Yes, I'm fine," she said as she closed the mirror, but not before tilting her head to take one last good look at Sebastein.

The young man's companions were disturbed by Sebastein's presence. They hadn't even seen him approaching their table. Sebastein stood there and glared at them without saying a word. Then he turned toward the young man in the wheelchair.

"What can we do for you?" asked one of the three men.

Sebastein was still focusing on the young man in the wheelchair, and without looking at the gentleman who was addressing him he responded. "Nothing, but maybe you can help him."

"Thanks for your concern, mister, but Hemingway is just fine."

"His bag needs changing and he is dying of thirst. Not even an animal deserves to be treated in this manner," replied Sebastein.

"Listen, mister, if Hemingway wants something he can ask for it, so why don't you mind your own business."

Before the gentleman could complete his thought, the lady who was with them spoke, "Look, Sam, he's right. Hemingway's bag does need changing and the battery in his voice activator must be dead, the light is off. No wonder he was so quiet, my poor baby."

Sebastein saw the sensitivity she displayed toward the young man in the wheelchair and sensed the sincerity within her voice. He turned to walk away but stopped when the lady, who apparently was the boy's mother, said, "Thank you for noticing our boy. But tell me, how did you know he had a bag at his side and that it was full? You couldn't have seen it under his clothing."

"I just had a hunch. Be sure and give him something to drink and change the battery on his voice activator," responded Sebastein as he continued on his way back to his table, where Monique waited anxiously.

"What happened?" asked Monique.

"Oh, nothing."

"For a moment I thought that man was going to hit you."

"No, nothing of the sort."

Monique and Sebastein picked up where they left off, revealing bits and pieces of their life experiences.

Half an hour later, Sebastein noticed that the young man in the wheelchair and his family were leaving. They all walked by his table without saying a word. As they reached the entrance to the restaurant, Sebastein was astonished when he heard "Thank you," coming from the young man's wheelchair. The young man's voice rang through the restaurant, distracting its customers momentarily. Sebastein got up from his chair and bowed to the young Caucasian male. Hemingway stared at Sebastein before his wheelchair was turned around to facilitate exit from the restaurant.

After dinner, Sebastein held Monique around the waist as they stood in front of the restaurant, waiting for the car to be brought up. All of a sudden, Sebastein loosened his embrace of Monique and held his stomach.

"Are you all right?" asked Monique.

"Yes, I am."

"Would you like me to drive?"

"That's not necessary."

The attendant brought the car up, and as they drove home the piercing pain returned. Sebastein held his stomach with one hand while trying to maintain control of the car. He didn't want to worry Monique so he tried desperately to hide the pain, which was growing more excruciating. A searing pain rushed through his side and without thinking, Sebastein released the steering wheel. The car began to swerve all over the road as

Monique tried desperately to keep it in control and in their lane. Sebastein's upper body jerked again in pain, but he was still conscious of the fact that he needed to stop the car. He jammed on the brakes, bringing the car to a complete stop.

"Something is definitely wrong," said Monique as she reached out to comfort Sebastein. He did not respond. A few minutes later, when the pain seemed to be slowly going away, he caught his breath, turned to Monique, and told her he was alright now.

"Was it something you ate?" she asked.

"Yes," he replied, knowing that the pain he felt was a sign that his time was coming. And although he knew this to be so, he did not want to alarm his beloved for fear that she would not understand. He slowly straightened and murmured, "I am alright now. Maybe it was just a little indigestion," he said as he started up the car and continued home.

When they arrived at Sebastein's gate, he noticed that Nick was waiting in his car across the street. "I see your friend is still there," Sebastein said.

Monique looked across the street and saw Nick's car. Nick's head bobbed up and down as he fought to stay awake. "I feel sorry for the poor fellow."

"So do I," said Sebastein.

Sebastein got out of the car and walked across the street to Nick's car. Sebastein banged on the car window. On the second knock, Nick straightened in his seat. He knew he'd been caught snoozing on the job. Nick slowly rolled down the car window.

When the window was halfway open, Sebastein said, "Monique will be here for a while, so why don't you follow me in. There is a room that you can use if you want. I can't imagine you would want to stay out here all night. You might break your neck trying to force yourself to stay awake."

"Don't mind if I do. Thank you very much, sir. I've been at it for forty-eight hours now without any sleep. By the way, where did you learn to drive like that? You drive like a wild man."

"Thank you. I'll take that as a compliment. Follow us in."

They drove in as Nick slowly followed. When they reached the doorway to Sebastein's home, Sebastein suddenly had another attack. He grabbed his stomach in pain as he tried to lean up against the pillar of his house. Monique and Nick rushed over to him. The front door opened and there stood Alimar with two other servants. Monique was somewhat amazed at their alertness; it was almost as if they were in tune with Sebastein. It was as if they knew when he was coming and when he was going, and the day and night began and ended with him.

Alimar told Monique and Nick that he and the other servants would take care of their master, but Monique insisted that she wanted to help. They took Sebastein inside, Nick following behind them. This time Monique was worried and extremely concerned about Sebastein's health and insisted on calling a doctor. But Alimar said no, and assured her that Sebastein would be okay because this had happened before.

Nick commented, "The poor man looks as if he is dying. Maybe he needs a doctor."

Monique agreed and said, "Yes, we should call a doctor."

But Alimar insisted that no doctor was necessary and this was reconfirmed by Sebastein who, in excruciating pain, said "No doctor is necessary. I just need some time to rest."

By now they had Sebastein sitting on the couch. While Monique and Nick were making sure that Sebastein was okay, Alimar rushed to the kitchen and soon after arrived with a solution. He gave it to Sebastein to drink, and Sebastein took the bottle from him and started to drink.

"What is that?" asked Monique.

"Something for the pain," replied Sebastein. He then told Alimar to show Nick to his room after he gave him something to eat. He assured Nick that Monique would be there in the morning.

Nick looked at Sebastein and said, "Thanks for everything, man, and I hope you feel alright."

Within fifteen minutes Sebastein started to feel better and it showed. Monique was relieved as she gently stroked his eyebrows and commented, "For a moment there I thought you were going to die."

Sebastein stared at her for a while and then replied, "With every death comes a new beginning and a new life, remember that." Monique attempted to say something, but Sebastein seemed to want to make sure that she understood what he was trying to say.

He continued, "Promise me that you will remember that with every death comes a new life and a beginning."

She knew there was some meaning to what he was saying, however, she did not understand. She replied, "I promise I will remember."

"Pain is a wonderful thing; it makes you realize how privileged you are to experience pleasure," said Sebastein.

They were interrupted by Alimar, who had come to check on the status of his master. Sebastein told him that he was well and that he should make sure that Nick was quite comfortable and had breakfast there in the morning. Alimar assured him that everything would be taken care of as usual. Monique and Sebastein said goodnight to a faithful friend as they went upstairs toward Sebastein's bedroom. Monique helped Sebastein to get undressed for bed. Before he went to bed, he uttered, "I love you so much, Monique."

"I love you, too, Sebastein." She tucked him in like a child and watched him drift off into a deep sleep.

Monique then tiptoed out of the room and went downstairs in the living room. She saw Alimar still closing up and completing his chores before going to bed. She asked him if he had a few minutes to spare, just to talk for a while, and he seemed pleased to do so. They sat on the couch and Monique began to ask him questions. "Has Sebastein seen a doctor for that pain before?"

"The master does not need to see a doctor, ma'am. He's fine," replied Alimar.

"How can you be so sure if he has never seen a doctor before? He looked as if he was in really bad pain. My God, man, for a moment there I thought he was going to die—and this was his second attack tonight."

Alimar took her hands as he responded, "I know you are very concerned, but the master is fine."

Monique's eyes were filled with tears as she said, "I hope you are right, Alimar, because I love him very much. It's silly, isn't it? Here I am in love with a man I don't even know."

"No, ma'am, it is not silly. Not at all."

"I don't even know where he is from, what he does for a living, nothing."

"Is it not enough that you love each other?"

"I suppose so. What did Sebastein mean when he said with every death comes a new beginning and a new life?" Before Alimar could answer, Monique continued to comment. "I got the impression he was trying to tell me something, almost as if there was a message. He was in extreme pain, but he wanted to make sure I understood that. What do you think it means?"

"I don't know, ma'am. Maybe it means that death is not the end of all things; rather it's a doorway to a new beginning."

"Maybe." She said goodnight to Alimar as she watched him walk away.

She then went to the kitchen in hopes that she could find the bottle that Sebastein drank from. She looked in the cupboard and other places but couldn't find it. As she was about to leave, she recognized the bottle sitting on a small shelf by itself. She picked it up and looked at it but she didn't see any label to show what was the potion within. She opened the bottle and put some on her fingertip in an attempt to taste it, but before she realized it, the substance from the bottle was cutting her skin and penetrating deeper and deeper into her flesh. She rushed toward the sink and washed off her finger while wondering what on earth such a solution was doing in the kitchen and what purpose it could serve.

When she looked at her finger closely, she noticed that the substance had peeled the skin off her fingertips. She was shocked when she saw the raw flesh beneath her skin and knew that the solution had the strength of acid. She was amazed to say the least that anyone could consume this solution internally and survive, and she concluded that it must have been the wrong bottle. She closed the bottle and put it back on the self, took some ice from the refrigerator and put it on her fingertip. Then she left the kitchen and went back upstairs in pain. A door in the huge mansion slowly closed and the eyes and ears of Alimar were no longer upon her.

Before going to bed, Monique took a Band-Aid from the medicine chest in the bathroom and covered the severe burn on her finger. She got into bed with Sebastein and snuggled up beside him, rested her head on his chest, and went to sleep. By now it was after midnight.

The night slowly drifted away into a bright and sunny morning. Monique woke up only find that she was all alone in the bed. Soon after she awoke, Sebastein entered the room in his jogging suit. She looked at him and was pleased because she could see that he was well again.

"I am glad that you are up and around. How do you feel?"

He sat on the bed beside her and responded, "I feel great."

"What time is it?"

"Almost noon."

"You must be joking. Is it really midday? Is it really that late?"

"Time is so unimportant when I am with you," Sebastein said as he leaned over and kissed her on the forehead.

Monique raised her hand in an attempt to touch his face and she noticed that there was no bandage on her finger and that her burn was completely healed. She sat up abruptly in the middle of the bed and looked at her finger.

"What happened?" she asked.

"What do you mean?"

"Last night I tried to taste the solution that I thought Alimar gave you to drink, to find out exactly what it was. Maybe I shouldn't have, but I did and got burned real badly.

It was like acid. I am sure I didn't dream that I got burnt, and now there is no burn. What's going on?"

"But that does not make sense. If I had drunk the solution that is as potent as you said, my God, I would be dead now."

"Well, I suppose you are right. I might have picked up the wrong bottle. The skin was practically peeled off the tip of my finger and I put a Band-Aid on it. I know I didn't dream it. What happened?"

Sebastein kissed her finger and again assured her that she was dreaming. "You see what happens when you worry too much about me."

Soon they were no longer discussing Monique's fingers but Sebastein's health again. "Are you sure you are alright?" asked Monique.

"Yes, yes, I am doing fine."

Monique told him that she was going to take a shower and asked if he would like to join her. He said no and humorously commented about saving his strength and she agreed. He told her that he would wait for her downstairs where they would have brunch together.

Sebastein then went back downstairs where he saw Nick walking around observing the different artworks on Sebastein's walls. "Do you like art?" asked Sebastein.

"I must say I do. But to be truthful, I don't know much about it."

"But it touches your heart and makes you like it. Too much emphasis is placed upon knowing; it is important that we accept things for what they are."

Nick gazed around Sebastein's mansion and commented, "This is some spread you have here. Must have cost you a fortune."

"It is an honor that you like it and find it as beautiful as I have. It is not necessary to put a price on that which is beautiful all the time."

Nick seemed indifferent to what Sebastein was trying to tell him and continued to talk away. "I don't know what you are doing, man, but keep doing it."

A few minutes later their conversation was interrupted by Monique, who walked into the room, gracing it with her presence. She said hello to Nick, went over to Sebastein and kissed him on the cheek. Sebastein signaled to Alimar that it was okay to serve brunch now, as he turned to Nick and asked if he would join them. Nick agreed while commenting how starved he was, hiding the fact that he'd had a helping earlier. They sat around the dining room table. As Monique's eyes caught the morning paper, she picked it up to scan the cover story. Her eyes opened wide as she gazed at the front page with lips moving slowly as she read to herself of the death of two policemen. She looked at their pictures in the paper and knew beyond any doubt that those were the two police officers who'd created the unpleasant experience for her and Sebastein. The paper said that the two officers' car had apparently run over a cliff and blown up, causing their deaths. But as Monique read on she looked at Sebastein, displaying doubts about how the officers had died.

She slowly went over to Sebastein, who by now was sitting around the table having his meal, and asked, "Did you see the morning paper?"

Sebastein took the paper from her and read the headlines. He handed back the paper to Monique and replied, "They must have angered the gods. Besides, when the standards of justice are violated by those who set them, then an act of injustice should not be questioned by those who betray them."

Monique threw the paper down on the dining room table and walked out angrily toward the stairs. Sebastein called her but she ignored him, and eventually found herself upstairs in their room. Sebastein told Nick to go ahead and have brunch, and that they would join him later. He went upstairs to talk to Monique. As Sebastein entered the room, he saw her still in a very angry state of mind. She stood there beside the bed with her hands folded and just looked at him with no words.

"Have I done or said something to offend you?" he asked calmly.

Monique did not respond. He moved closer to her and attempted to put his hand on her shoulder. She stepped back frightened of him. He could see that she was obviously upset but lacked the words to comfort her. He turned and walked toward the door, stopped, and held the door handle.

As he opened the door halfway, she asked in a very curious way, "Who are you, Sebastein? Who are you really?"

Sebastein, with his back still turned toward her, responded, "I am Sebastein, the man you are supposed to be in love with, remember?"

Monique, overwhelmed with emotions, started to cry as she said, "You know, someone once said, Sebastein, that love without respect is like a flower without water. Soon it will fade away and die. It is obvious that you do not respect me. Maybe it is because you think I am this naive young kid who is totally unaware of everything. I saw something last night that I tried to ignore, then this morning the two officers who offended you and I are now dead. That was no accident, was it, Sebastein?"

"No."

As he again attempted to leave, he looked at her and said softly, "I respect you and I love you. Please forgive me for what I have done. Yes, I am responsible for their deaths, but their actions dictated the sentence. I've no regrets for my action."

"But how? You were with me. How did you do it?" asked Monique.

"How is not important. What is important is that they will never treat anyone like that again."

"You're like ice."

Without commenting on Monique's remark, Sebastein went back downstairs and soon found himself in his garden, sitting on the ground, where he began to meditate.

Meanwhile, upstairs, Monique gathered her belongings and came storming down the stairs. She saw Nick sitting there feeding his face and said angrily to him, "Is my father paying you to eat or is he paying you to take care of me? I would like to leave right now."

Nick got up immediately, with his mouth still filled with food, and walked outside. They got into his car and drove off Sebastein's estate without saying good-bye.

As Sebastein sat there in the garden, with his legs folded in a lotus position, he knew that Monique was leaving and by now had gone out of his reach, but he did not know what to do. After that day two weeks passed by, during which neither of them tried to get in touch with the other. Yet each of them was going through their own private torment because they longed for each other. Because of pride, they struggled to stay apart, almost as if it were a struggle that each of them must win.

8

As the woman who was jogging on the beach got farther and farther away, Sebastein snapped back to the present. He realized he was still standing on the beach. He looked around and saw that his dogs were still standing beside him like sentinels. Sebastein headed home to rest because he had become exhausted from the memories.

It had been three months now and still no form of communication between him and Monique. It seemed as if Sebastein indulged in his own private solitude, often with his two friends, the German shepherds, while at the Ryans' home, Monique tried to forget a man whom she loved more strongly as time went by. She tried to drown her sorrow by engaging in constant shopping with Charlene, and attending different parties almost every night. Still those things were not enough to fill the emptiness within her. Although she was surrounded by family and friends who loved her very much, she was still lonely. Each morning she took up the phone to call Sebastein but found herself putting it down before she finished dialing. Both lovers were miserable and still they were determined to stay apart.

Alimar grew concerned for his master's health, for he knew that in a couple of months his master would die, and this thought weighed heavily on his mind. He approached Sebastein in his humble fashion and asked him, "Master, should I call her?"

Sebastein replied, "It is not time, Alimar, my good friend. When the time comes you will know, and so will she."

Alimar bowed down before him then slowly departed, leaving Sebastein to continue his meditation.

*   *   *

Two more weeks went by. It was Saturday morning and it was business as usual at the Ryans' home, except this was supposed to be a very special morning for a young woman who had lost weight and grown petite from feelings that she could not control. At about ten o'clock that Saturday morning there was a knock at the Ryans' door. Ben, in his usual fashion, went to see who it was. He opened the door and saw an elderly man with a turban around his head, looking as if he had lived in the desert all his life.

Ben, in his snobbish way, asked, "May I help you, sir?"

"I am here to see Monique," replied the elderly man.

"Do come in," said Ben. Sebastein had apparently grown on him for now he was not afraid to let an unknown Black indoors.

"Thank you," replied the elderly man.

Ben went and got Monique, and as she approached the living room she was surprised to see Alimar. She walked over, thinking it was a mirage as she hugged him and asked how he was doing. Alimar was glad to see that she still remembered him.

"Very well, ma'am," replied Alimar. "But don't you mean how is my master doing?"

"I suppose I do. How is he doing, Alimar?"

"Why did you leave my master?"

She stepped away from Alimar, hanging her head as she played nervously with a rubber band. "Love consumes; part of being in love is knowing when to walk away."

Alimar walked closer to her as if he wanted to see her reaction. He told her, "My master is dying." He saw the reaction that for some reason he knew would be there.

When Monique looked at him she was about to faint. She held her mouth, "No, it can't be, no."

"I am sorry," said Alimar, "but he is dying. I am here without his knowledge because I would like you to go to him and make his remaining days as happy as only you can."

74

"The pain he felt that night when we went out together, is it part of the symptoms?"

"Yes, I suppose you could say it is part of the illness as you know it to be."

"How long have you known that Sebastein was dying?"

"I have always known."

Monique shook her head in confusion and said, "I don't understand. Why didn't he say something?"

"Will you go to him now?"

"What makes you think he wants to see me?"

Alimar took her hands and said, "I know, I know."

She felt some form of reassurance and promised Alimar that she would see him. They said goodbye and Monique walked with him to the door, but before he could leave she asked out of curiosity, "How did you know where to find me?"

Alimar remarked, "Your bodyguard Nick seems to like our kitchen."

Monique forced a brief smile and said, "Oh, I see." They said their good-byes again as she watched him get into his car and drive off.

Later that day, Monique saw Nick walking idly around the yard. As she approached him with an angry look on her face, he became worried but was pleased when she leaned over and kissed him on the mouth. "Thank you, Nick," she said as she turned and went back inside the house. Nick knew what that kiss was for and with a big smile on his face he continued to walk idly around the yard.

Monique had planned to visit Sebastein the next morning, but she grew very anxious and could not wait. It was now about 5:00 P.M., and she told her chauffeur to get the car ready because she would like to go somewhere. She called Sebastein's estate and Alimar answered the phone; she told him she was on her way over. Alimar sounded pleased and promised that he would let her in when she reached the gate. Within an hour's time, Monique was at Sebastein's mansion.

Meanwhile Sebastein was in the garden doing his daily meditation. His meditation was interrupted by a familiar scent. It was Monique, and he knew it. He opened his eyes, turned around quickly, and saw her standing there. Without a word, he went and grabbed her around the waist, picked her up, and hugged her tightly as she reciprocated the warmth. They expressed how glad they were to see each other, but soon became very formal.

"How are you?" she asked Sebastein.

"I am doing well."

"Are you really?"

"Yes. Why did you come?"

"I don't know. Maybe it is because I missed you. Why didn't you tell me?"

"You mean that I am dying? Is that the only reason you are here?"

"I am here because I love you."

"Do you truly love me?"

"With all my heart."

"Then marry me."

Monique hesitated, turned, and walked away for a while as if she was trying to compose herself after another mindbuster. She turned around and said, "How can I marry a man I don't even know, a man I won't be able to spend the rest of my life with? Sebastein, I really don't know if I can marry you. But I really do know that I love you. If only you could help me to understand. Help me to know you better."

Sebastein turned his back to her. "You ask me who I am, which is an old, familiar question I have heard for the past two thousand years. If I told you who I am you would not believe it. Therefore it is best that you accept me for who you think I am."

Monique started to cry. "Please don't do this to me, Sebastein, please don't. Can't you see that I love you?"

He went closer to her and wiped her tears. Then he sat, closing his eyes then opening them. Seconds later he looked at her and said, "Two thousand years ago I was crucified on Calvary. Although I was proclaimed dead, I rose on the third day and ascended to the heavens but did not stay. Little does mankind know that after I fulfilled my Father's prophesy it was also the beginning not only for the entire human race but also for myself. For they are under the delusion that I am somewhere beyond the sky getting ready to return like a thief in the night. Little do they know that the Comforter the Father had sent them from the beginning is still here among them, where I must be conceived and be born, and rise on the third day fulfilling my Father's prophesy again until it's time to die. For if this does not come to pass humanity will have lost its mediator between heaven and all the iniquity that has plagued the earth."

By now Monique was sitting and listening intently to Sebastein as he spoke.

He continued, "At times I am angry with my Father and have placed him with the collection of unworthy gods, for he led me to believe that my suffering and pain would end on the cross at Calvary. Little did I know that it was within my destiny to walk the earth like a human. Yes, that is one of the many wishes of my Father, a god who has ruled for centuries and developed a temperament that is no longer suited for the delivery of justice."

"Are you saying what I think you are saying? Are you saying that you are the Christ?"

"Yes."

"But you are . . ."

Sebastein finished the sentence. "I know, I am black. It seems like yesterday when a generation of people asked themselves a similar question. How can a carpenter's son, a man who was born in a stable, be the son of God?" He stared at Monique and continued, "The son of man deals not with the body but with the spirit."

Monique got up, held her head in confusion and then said, "I don't know what to say. I don't even know what is the truth anymore."

Sebastein replied, "The truth is a relative concept ready to become known to those who are already a part of it. Therefore seek not to know the truth but what is not, for by doing so you shall be at one with that which is already a part of you."

"This is too much," she said shaking her head with her hands in the air. "The Christ here with me. This is just too much, too much to believe. What about all this killing and murdering, and all the things that are making our lives miserable? How do you fit into it?" she asked angrily.

Sebastein got up, looked at her and said, "The crucifixion of the body is an enlightenment to the soul, for as the moon bears testimony to the night and not the day so will our suffering bear testimony to our soul and not our body."

"I don't know what you mean by that. But why would the son of man stand by and watch his people suffer and turn his back against them? Tell me that, Sebastein, if you are the Christ."

"The son of man has always been here for his people. It is they who have isolated themselves from me by creating an image of an entity that does not coincide with the teaching and the beliefs of my father. They claim that I died and went to heaven and must walk a road of tribulation until my return. But what they fail to understand is that I came back and I have always been here."

Monique shook her head again and said, "You are asking me to believe that you, the man I slept with, are the son of God."

Sebastein looked at her and said, "I have yet to unravel the mystery of my father's mind. Though for centuries I have convinced myself that my destiny truly lies in the hands of God and not in the bosom of men, now I am faced with the harsh reality again that if the prophesy is to come through you must play your role, for you have been chosen."

"But why should I even think about marrying you, Sebastein, when you won't be around to hold me and spend the rest of your life with me? Why?"

"Because you are part of my destiny," Sebastein said softly. "And though I would fight the demons in what you call hell and denounce all the angels in Heaven to spend a lifetime in your arms, I must prepare myself for the day I return to my father's kingdom."

"Those officers, the policemen who stopped us, how and what did you do to ensure their deaths?"

"Even the God of love and mercy can be angered by the scum of the earth."

"But if you are the Messiah then they are your children."

"Each man has two channels, one that leads to God and one that leads to Lucifer. We must choose our own path, Monique. And when those officers did what they did to you, they sealed their fate. Yes, it was their time, just like within a month from now it will be my time."

Monique looked at the finger that had been burned by the solution in the bottle from the kitchen and said curiously, "So I did not dream or imagine that I got burned on my finger."

Sebastein smiled and said, "No."

She looked at her finger, which had no scar tissue and had perfectly healed. "Part of me wants to believe you, Sebastein. But I don't know. I need a little time to think things through."

"You have a few weeks because my time is coming to an end now."

"But if you are the Christ, why don't you save yourself?"

Sebastein stared at her and knew that two thousand years ago he had heard those same words on the cross from a man beside him.

Monique held her mouth and came to the realization that from her biblical teachings she too had doubted and had followed the same path as one of the men who was nailed to the cross. "My God. I can't believe I said that. Those were basically the same words the man said to the Christ on the cross, weren't they?"

Sebastein did not respond. She turned and started to walk away, saying that she needed some time to think. She had to get away. Sebastein called at her. She turned around and looked at him.

"Listen to your heart, Monique; listen to your heart and not to your reason."

She left Sebastein, who continued to meditate as if he had not been interrupted. And as he sat there being at peace with himself and the universe, he knew she would struggle within herself to come to the understanding of an enigma that she would never be able to comprehend. But he also knew that, like him, she had no control over what was destined to be. Sebastein sat there with his eyes closed, and suddenly his entire body began jerking in a feverish manner. He opened his eyes quickly, startled to find himself face to face with an ancient entity who appeared in the gender of a woman.

"Mother, you remember," he said with tears running down his face. He was quiet for a while, as if he was listening, then he continued to speak. "Help her to find the peace within herself and to understand that it is not by my wish, but by that of our Heavenly Father." He opened his fist, which was clenched tightly, and saw blood running between his fingers though there was no apparent wound.

Meanwhile, back on the beach, a confused and troubled woman walked the shore as Nick, who sensed that she needed to be alone, stayed a distance from her. She stayed on the beach for about forty-five minutes before rushing back to her home, and not before long she was rushing out again. Soon, Monique found herself at the home of Father Andreas. She rang the bell several times but there was no answer. As she attempted to leave the door was opened by her dear friend Father Andreas.

"Monique, is that really you?" he asked happily.

"Yes, Father," she replied. They embraced and went inside to the living room.

Father Andreas, a 48-year-old bishop of the Roman Catholic Church, expressed again how happy he was to see her. "What brings you to my humble place?" Father Andreas asked.

"Your good looks, of course," replied Monique jokingly.

"If I were fifteen years younger, I would give all those young bucks a run for their money."

"Are you kidding? I am sure you have all the girls running after you right now. Father," Monique asked, becoming serious, "Do you believe that Jesus Christ is alive today?"

The bishop looked at her, surprised by the question. "Within my teaching I must believe that Jesus is alive and sitting on the right hand of God."

"Is it possible that he is here on earth and walking among us right now, this day?" Monique asked anxiously.

"I don't think so, my child. The Bible tells us that when he returns, he will return so everybody will know. It will be the day of judgement, as I am sure you know. What has gotten into you, Monique? Why all these questions?"

"What happens if he came back and stayed?"

"What are you getting at, my child?"

"What if when he was crucified and rose on the third day, he ascended into Heaven, came back soon thereafter, and remained on earth to help mankind. Is that possible, Father?"

"Well, anything is possible, my child. What makes you so sure that he returned to earth?"

She got up and apologized to Father Andreas for disturbing him and insisted that she must be going. She reached the door and Father Andreas walked over, took her by the shoulder, and led her back to the couch.

"I have known you since you were a teenager. You have always been curious. What I sense now is more than curiosity. Is there something you want to tell me?"

"I met a man who claims to be the Christ."

"Well it's not a surprise because every day of late someone is claiming to be the Christ. You remember Jim Jones and David Koresh."

"You don't understand. This is a person whom I know and for some reason I am beginning to believe that he is the Christ. I know you probably think I am losing my mind, but if you met this man you would know what I am talking about Father."

"Well, why don't we?" asked Father Andreas.

81

"What do you mean?" replied Monique.

"Let's go and meet this man who claims to be the Messiah."

Monique was startled at the suggestion and said maybe it wasn't such a good idea. But Father Andreas persuaded her and told her that if the Messiah was among men he would not take offense to talking to one of his humble servants. Monique decided that maybe the Father was right. She promised to take Father Andreas the next morning to Sebastein's place. Father Andreas kissed her on the forehead, blessed her, and promised that he would be ready when she came to pick him up the next morning and together they would go to see the self-proclaimed Messiah.

9

Father Andreas was up at the crack of dawn. He had hardly slept that night, thinking about his conversation with Monique. It was not that he believed for one minute that the Messiah was here on earth. After all, Christ has been sitting on the right hand of his Father for over two thousand years. Father Andreas was concerned about the impact the stranger's story was having on Monique. She was like a daughter to him and he did not want to see her faith shattered. For Monique's sake he knew he would have to tread carefully with the stranger. The thought of conducting an exorcism brought a smile to Father Andreas' face, but he knew that was not an option because someone with a delusion of that magnitude would not easily succumb.

Father Andreas was standing by his front door when Monique pulled up. He got into the passenger seat and Monique sped off. They drove for a few minutes in silence.

"Monique, I was thinking. Perhaps it would be better if I were to meet with this gentleman alone. Perhaps he will be a little more revealing since he will be talking to a man of the cloth."

"I think that would be a good idea. I'll find some excuse so that the two of you can be alone."

There was silence again between the two, then Father Andreas spoke. "I gather this man is more than a friend."

Monique looked at him and knew from the bottom of her heart that she could not deceive him. "Yes."

"Whoever this man is, he must have you very convinced that he is the Christ because I have never seen you so shaken up before."

"Love does strange things to a person, Father. I feel as if I am locked in a struggle of the supreme beings. Sometimes I think I'm unworthy to be a part of God's kingdom and yet if there is a hell I don't think I deserve to go there. Where do I belong?"

'I don't know what to say, my child, except that I would like to believe that each of us has a special niche carved out in the universe. Where that place is, only God knows."

It was 11:00 A.M. when they reached Sebastein's mansion. Sebastein had returned from his daily walk with his dogs and was again in the garden, meditating. It was as if time had stood still and the garden was his only place of refuge. He sat there as if the entire world was again on his shoulders.

"Master, you have visitors," Alimar interrupted.

With his eyes still closed Sebastein replied, "I know. Show them to the garden."

Father Andreas and Monique walked into the garden, where Sebastein was still sitting with his eyes closed. Monique felt awkward, not knowing what explanation she was going to give Sebastein for bringing Father Andreas.

"Welcome to my humble abode," Sebastein said as he got up from the ground.

"Father Andreas, meet Sebastein. Sebastein, this is Father Andreas. He's an old friend of the family."

"I know," replied Sebastein. Sebastein then stroked her cheek with his right hand and kissed her softly on the lips as he whispered, "Oh woman of little faith."

Monique smiled because she did not know how to take his comment, but she remained composed as the atmosphere became strained by the intensity of emotions that were generating among the three people in the garden. The silence between them was becoming overbearing, so Monique felt this was the perfect time to make her escape. "I must have my morning coffee before I do anything. I think I'll go and see what Alimar has in stock. I'm sure you two have a lot to talk about until I return."

After Monique left, Sebastein sat back on the ground and closed his eyes. Father Andreas thought this was quite strange if not downright impolite. Then again he didn't know if Sebastein's action was some strange cultural tradition of which he was not aware.

Sebastein opened his eyes for a split second before closing them again. But in that brief moment he had familiarized himself with the gentleman who stood before him with a third of his Irish whiskey still left in the flask tucked neatly away beneath his robe. The aroma could still be detected from his beard. His receding hairline and obvious birthmark in the middle of his head, somewhat like Gorbachev's, was showing through the few strands of hair that were combed into the spot in a failed attempt to hide his baldness.

Father Andreas moved, trying to keep his weight off his right foot, where he had a corn sticking out on his smallest toe. Refusing to see a podiatrist because it was cheaper to put a razor to it himself, he guarded the toe from harm's way as if it was the royal jewel.

"Ask your questions, priest, now that you have achieved your purpose of making sure that we are alone," Sebastein said.

Father Andreas was momentarily startled and for the first few seconds did not know how to respond. "Well, I must admit, I wanted some time to talk to you alone. I have been hearing some strange things about you, and you can't blame someone in my position for being a little curious. You understand, don't you?"

Sebastein whispered softly, "I do."

"Mr. Sebastein, it would appear that we both love Monique very much. I must say, however, that she seems very confused and I am concerned about her state of mind. Needless to say, I believe a great deal of it has a lot to do with what you told her. May I ask why are you doing this to someone you claim to love?"

"Trouble not yourself, priest, for blessed is she amongst women. And as time goes by her burden will get lighter and lighter."

"Forgive my bluntness, Mr. Sebastein, but I have been told that you have proclaimed yourself the son of God."

"We're all God's children," replied Sebastein with his head hung as he remained in his lotus position.

"Indeed, but not all of us go around calling ourselves the Christ, the savior and keeper of our redemption."

"I have led you to the path of redemption, but I have never promised to be its keeper. That choice lies in your hands."

"Blasphemy!" said Father Andreas angrily to Sebastein. "If you are whom you said you are, how about a little miracle. Nothing fancy. Maybe walk on water. That's one you should be quite skilled with."

"How typical that everything that is associated with God has to be a miracle. A miracle is nothing but an unexpected gift from God to some who think themselves unworthy or lack the insight to see why the gift is being given. I tell you this, the son of man did not come to perform like a monkey on a tightrope to convince humanity of his existence."

Father Andreas started to say something but hesitated. Soon after that out it came. "If you so need to indulge in your delusion of grandeur, I imagine that is your business. But a young woman whom I have watched grow up is confused because of the nonsense you're filling her head with."

"When emotions begin to sway and doubts begin to set in, look toward the heart for comfort."

"My heart is not as innocent as a young woman who is apparently in love with you."

"Perhaps that is the problem."

"Come on, I am not some poor slob you can feed this crap. I am a learned man and I have been studying and preaching the gospel for many years now."

"Intelligence is nothing unless you have the wisdom to use it wisely. Priest, why do you seek to anger me? Is it because I am who I am?"

"You mean who you *say* you are."

"The first step to true wisdom is to acknowledge one's ignorance of all things. Open your heart and empty your mind, priest."

"But if you are the Christ, what are you doing here in this garden? You should be out there letting people know that you have returned and carrying out the promises that you have made in the Scriptures. Your fame by now should know no boundary—that is, of course, if you *are* the Christ."

"Fame is being respected and admired by others for sharing a part of yourself with humanity. This I have done already before and after my resurrection. I have always been here, living day by day, fulfilling the prophesy. Now, once again, my death is near. Through my death a troubled world will once again find peace within itself. But if you mean why is it that I have not taken my followers and ascended up into the heavens, this will only come to pass when the son of man has made his final ascent to the heavens and taken his rightful place beside his father. But until then, we must all live until it's time to die."

Father Andreas scratched his beard as he said to Sebastein, "There is a question I have always wanted to ask the Messiah or someone whom I thought would possibly know the answer. Would you mind very much if I asked you that question, Mr. Sebastein?"

Knowing Father Andreas's thoughts, Sebastein asked, "What teaching or denomination is closest to the heavenly Father's wishes?"

Father Andreas looked at Sebastein and for a moment thought his heart had stopped, for that was indeed the question. Then he began to look at Sebastein in a different light, as if just maybe, for a second or two, all doubt had wiped away from his face.

"How did you know that? How did you know that would be the question?"

"Any teaching that puts my father in the center will lead to the path to God's kingdom. But only if that teaching recognizes the son of man as the one and only Messiah, for as you are well aware, I am the only way to God's kingdom. For since I have soiled myself in the iniquity of my people's sins I must cleanse them before they are worthy to touch the ground that my Father walks on."

"Very interesting," said Father Andreas. "But I am troubled because there is a population of people, of which I am sure you are aware, from the Jewish descent, who reject the Christ. Are you saying that they will not see your Father's kingdom?"

"Maybe they know of another way to my Father's kingdom. All are welcome in my Father's kingdom. But only if they recognize my name."

Father Andreas responded, "I have doubts, and I must admit sometimes I feel unworthy because of these doubts. But when I look around and see so many people dying from cancer, AIDS, and the many forms of pestilence, I wonder. Young infants who have not yet lived are plagued by more afflictions than we are able to find cures for. Sometimes I blame our creator for not doing anything about it. I know I shouldn't, but I do."

"Which creator?" interjected Sebastein.

"Which creator? There is only one God, isn't there?" asked Father Andreas, who was disappointed in Sebastein's question.

"Indeed, but there are two creators," replied Sebastein as the windows of both men's souls embraced each other.

"You're right, of course. Jesus himself is our creator in his own right," said Father Andreas with a smile.

"I, my Father, and our creator the living God are all one," said Sebastein.

Father Andreas seemed confused, and for a moment his search for this unknown creator brought a blank look on his face. "Then to whom do you refer as our creator besides God?"

Sebastein took a hard, long look at Father Andreas, then replied, "Lucifer."

"How dare you speak of Lucifer in the same light as our creator?" asked Father Andreas angrily.

"How dare you not? You speak of diseases that eat away at the human flesh, stripping us of our dignity, having little or no regard for the innocent. To whom do you attribute these things?"

Father Andreas was silent as Sebastein answered his own question. "Yes, the mischievous creator, Lucifer, spokesman for the laws of circumstance. Many do not understand that there are two creators. One is the creator of all things, the other is the creator of the variations of all things. Be aware of the mischievous creator, for his purpose is real. He serves to model the living God as only he can in such a way that the purpose and the meaningfulness of man's existence will often be confounded by his inability to make a clear distinction between what rules should govern his life. This mischievous creator will always create an illusion based on reality with the primary function to distract, strengthening the essence of his master plan, which is the format for his opposition. Listen, and listen well, for unless you are one with the spirit of the Messiah you will never be able to see the fine line that separates the realm of his creations from God's, for they appear one and the same."

Father Andreas shook his head and went on to another question, "When you speak of yourself as the Messiah, should it be taken figuratively or literally?"

Sebastein remembered the story of who should cast the first stone and gazed around as if he was looking for an answer in the elements of the universe, then he said, "I claim that you do not disclaim all possibilities, whether they fall in the realm of your comprehension or not."

"I believe that we are all God's children, but some of us need more guidance than others. Not to dwell on the Jews, but they have rejected Christ and they have refused to accept him, how . . ."

"Did they?" interrupted Sebastein.

Father Andreas was silent once again, then replied, "Yes."

"Is it that they have rejected Christ or the idea that they think he has placed himself above God? They did not reject me; they have merely placed my Heavenly Father above me. They do not understand that because of man's sins they can never become one with God unless they have cleansed themselves through me. Though there are many paths to the holy circle, there is only one door, and I alone hold the key."

"But is this not arrogance on their part?"

"Perhaps, or perhaps one of the greatest expressions of love."

"How can this be when God the Father, God the Son and God the Holy Ghost are all the embodiment of the living God? To reject one is to reject all, for together they function as one."

"Why must the holy trinity come together as one in order to function in its highest capacity? Is it not enough that each entity reaches the epitome of homeostasis within its respective domain? Will not the same purpose be served? Maybe the Jews have simply borne testimony to this doctrine."

"Why are you so partial to them?"

"And why are you so angry at them?"

"Hell, the world has reason to be. They crucified the son of the living God. I am surprised you are not."

"For a man of the cloth, you hold very narrow-minded views."

Father Andreas became a bit annoyed and started to walk away.

"Why was the Christ crucified?" asked Sebastein.

Father Andreas stopped, "Because he claimed to be the son of God."

"But was that not evident by his deeds? When you think of my crucifixion, think of me as a casualty of war, a war for the domination of religious and political ideologies. Do not be deceived: I was not crucified because I was the son of God. There were men before me who had proclaimed themselves prophets and even the Christ, yet they remained untouched. No, my death was a necessity, for my very presence represented a threat to the hierarchy within a social system, a social system that could not stand the fact that I was breathing new ideas into the hearts of men, raising their consciousness and allowing them to feel and think differently about things that were considered the status quo. He who dares to speak what others will only think will always be viewed as a rebel amongst the flock. Blame no one for my death; relinquish your hate as you welcome other countries which were once your enemies—so must you learn to display love and understanding to people who acted as they must in times of war."

Father Andreas's built-up anger found an outlet. "You do not deserve the greatness of God's love, much less to equate yourself with the Messiah." His words struck a nerve in Sebastein.

Sebastein's eyes opened quickly as an infuriating rage flashed across his face, one that even the twelve-foot aquarium with tiny species of fishes gazing at him through the glass could not calm. Within moments he was up on his feet, his reaction swift as he grabbed Father Andreas's walking stick, which this priest used to shift his weight to ease the pain from the callus on his toe. Using the stick, Sebastein smashed the twelve-foot aquarium, sending the water and fishes flooding to the ground.

Meanwhile, Father Andreas, who had lost his balance when Sebastein grabbed his third leg, found himself in the middle of the garden, crashing down on Sebastein's tulips, all the time trying to prevent his fall from hurting the callus.

Sebastein looked at him fiercely while the fish continued to flap around at his feet, gasping, out of their element. "The greatness of my Father's love? What do you know about the greatness of my Father's love?"

"Easy, Mr. Sebastein. I did not mean to offend you. I merely meant—"

"Shut up!" yelled Sebastein, cutting off Father Andreas' thought. "If God's love was so wonderful, why didn't he die for your sins rather than send me? Whose love can be greater? The one who allowed himself to be sacrificed or the one who sent the lamb to the slaughter? I tell you this, I questioned God's love with every stroke of the soldier's hammer and my love for him died a little each time the nails pierced my flesh, finding their destination in the wooden cross."

Father Andreas nervously spoke. "Surely you do not think that our Lord did not want to die for our sins, Mr. Sebastein?"

"If the truth be known, I did not die for the sins of humanity."

"For what other reason did you die?" asked Father Andreas, who had decided to humor Sebastein in hopes of calming him.

"The love of my Father."

"I do not understand."

"Like so many children in this world, I too have always wanted my Father's approval. I guess you could say that I had become an emotional prisoner, one who was willing to die for his Father's approval. When the opportunity presented itself I gladly capitalized on the chance to win his love."

"I cannot imagine God not loving his only son, who has done him proud."

"It is not that he didn't love me, but rather his love for the world was greater."

"Forgive me, Mr. Sebastein. At the risk of offending you, but you sound like a jealous child in competition for his father's love."

"What child does not crave for the love of a father?"

"The question as to why God himself did not die for our sins did not cross my mind, perhaps because I have always viewed you and your Father as one. But it's a valid one, isn't it?"

"It goes to reasons."

"But what's the answer?"

Sebastein had become totally subdued and rational by now. "Although Lucifer got exactly what he deserved, the lesson at hand is that God does not like to answer the same question twice, as was obvious by his reluctance to reveal the secret of breathing life into man."

"You mean he was asked once before as to why he himself did not die for the sins of humanity?"

"Yes!"

"By whom?"

"By me, of course!"

"And what was his answer?"

"One was not given, but after two thousand years I have finally figured out the answer."

"May I inquire about your speculation?"

"It is one you may choose not to believe."

"No offense, Mr. Sebastein, but I don't think my day could get any weirder based on anything else you might say."

"I know it's hard, but the ultimate confrontation is facing the truth that we spend half our lives trying to fool ourselves. Consider this an opportunity not to be fooled by what you were conditioned to believe."

"So why, Mr. Sebastein? Why do you think God chose not to die for the sins of humanity?"

"Because the greatest gift he has ever given to man, ironically, is the only one he cannot give to himself."

"God's greatest gift to man is life, am I right?"

"Yes."

"Then surely a God who gives life so abundantly cannot be lacking."

"If the death of God ever became a reality, resurrection would not be at hand."

"God is eternal. Everybody knows he cannot die."

"But he can, and if he does he would not be able to resurrect himself. This is the irony: that he alone holds the secret of breathing life into man but should he die he would not be able to breathe life into himself. Hence he chose me to die, for he knew he would be able to give me life again."

"The Bible teaches us that God is eternal and will never die. Now I ask you, Mr. Sebastein, what on earth or in Heaven could penetrate his armor and subject him to such human frailties?"

"Exposure!" replied Sebastein as he glared at Father Andreas.

"Exposure? Exposure to what?"

"To sin."

"Then it would seem, Mr. Sebastein, that if indeed exposure to sin would mean the death of our creator, surely you cannot blame him for not wanting to die for the sins of humanity, especially since the world would die with him."

"I love my Father and do not blame him for anything. Still, I often wonder why he did not trust me enough to share the gift of breathing life into man."

"But it has been written that man has been resurrected from the dead because of you."

"Not because of me. I was only an instrument through which his power flows. No, like Lucifer I was never privy to that information. It's a secret I think he will never reveal to anyone else."

The conversation took a turn as Father Andreas continued to probe. Suddenly Father Andreas realized that his walking stick was in his hand. He looked at it closely wondering when he might have picked it up because he couldn't remember. He shook his head and was about to continue the conversation when he noticed that the aquarium was back to normal. The fishes were no longer on the ground but in their watery environment, swimming around as if they had never been disturbed. "How? How did—?"

Sebastein interrupted, "Why should their world be destroyed because a pebble was dropped in mine?"

"But how? When?" Father Andreas asked as he walked closer to inspect the aquarium, all the time wondering how strange it was to have an aquarium in the garden. After all, no one puts an aquarium in a garden.

Before Father Andreas could raise another question, Sebastein walked over to him, placed his hands on his shoulders as if they were old friends and said, "You mentioned the Jews. All men are welcome into my Father's kingdom, for even a young man who has indulged in homosexuality, who is guilty of being a sodomite, can be forgiven by the son of man. Even he can enter the kingdom of God for his sins are forgiven."

Father Andreas' face turned red as a beet, for he knew he was the one who had indulged in such an act, and he could see the gentleness within Sebastein's eyes and the forgiveness behind them. He knew that no one knew of the secret, except he and his God, and another man who had vowed to be silent, and that man had been dead for years. Father Andreas knew that Sebastein had to be the Messiah to know the things that he did. He fell to his knees and worshipped Sebastein, as tears fell down his beard.

"Forgive me once again."

Sebastein held Father Andreas by his shoulders, raised him to his feet, and whispered, "I forgave you even before you asked for my forgiveness. For although the past never goes away, rather hides behind the present and the future, I am empowered by my Father to erase it. For in the eyes of the gods we are all like little angels with horns." Suddenly they realized that Monique was present.

"What's going on?" asked Monique as she looked and saw Father Andreas sobbing. "What have you done to him, Sebastein?"

Father Andreas interrupted, "No, my child, you do not understand, he has to be the Christ."

Monique was startled by his remark and felt a little better that she was not alone in this realm of madness, in thinking that Sebastein was the Christ.

Sebastein walked over to her and said, "I know it is unnatural to clip the wings of a butterfly, but as Mary played her role two thousand years ago so must you indulge my heavenly Father and bear testimony to the prophesy that will give birth to an old concept that needs to be revived in the hearts of men."

"I still need more time," said Monique.

"I know. And regardless of what you may think of me, I do love you."

Monique sighed, then replied, "I don't know, it's like I am in love with two different people. On one hand, I am in love with Sebastein the romantic, exciting fellow. On the other hand, I am afraid to touch the other side because I think I may not be worthy to do so. I must admit that you mystify me. I suppose that you know the exact day that you are going to die, don't you?" asked Monique.

"Yes. But remember, with every death comes a new life and a new beginning."

Monique smiled and said, "I knew the first time you said those words to me that you were trying to tell me something. I just didn't know what, but now I do know. I know I need more time to think, Sebastein. If it is God's wish that I do the things you ask of me, then I should be honored and consider myself very fortunate, and I will. It's just that I never thought the son of God would be my soul mate."

"The son of man is no one's soul mate; neither are you."

Monique was a little bit taken back by Sebastein's response and sought to explore his thoughts to ascertain whether or not he meant she was only an object being made to play a role in his destiny. Sebastein's response intensified her doubts and splashed her insecurities across her heart. "I'm sorry. I guess with all this happening I some way along the line developed the idea that we were probably meant to be with each other. Silly me," Monique responded sarcastically.

Sebastein stepped closer to her and held her hands. "Your hands are so cold. You're trembling. Do not be distraught by my words. I merely meant that although we are destined to be together the phrase 'soul mate' is often so misleading."

"Don't you believe that for every man there is a woman and vice versa, and that both were meant to be together?"

"Souls can be mated before birth but split apart at birth. Having been a part of God's holy circle, it is inevitable that souls are joined."

"Why do we give up our ability to find our soul mates at birth?"

"It is not by choice that we do this, but that when we come into existence as 'tabula rasa' the purity that comes with this state is defiled by the learning experiences in our environment."

"So we were only soul mates in the presence of God's holy circle, and once we are born the process is clouded because of the things we learn, which is why we think, feel, and act differently from one another?"

"Yes, but even more importantly, it is because each person's learning experience is so distinct that the link is broken. Think of this, if soul mates were meant to exist after birth, why didn't our heavenly Father implant a sign or mark uniquely designed for us to recognize each other as opposed to making us wonder whether or not we are marrying Mr. or Ms. Right.

Surely with all his creations such a task would have been a simple one."

"I suppose it would have been."

"The phrase 'soul mate' implies that our souls have gender. This concept exists only in the minds of man. Monique, you are a beautiful woman, but your gender emerges as a result of conception. Before conception you were only an entity whose light served to make God's holy circle more complete. When you die your gender dies with you; it does not become an extension of your soul."

"Listening to you one would believe that when we face our heavenly Father it will not be as men or women."

"There will come a time when we'll have no choice but to leave our earthly and bodily qualities behind. The gender that served to help us in the act of procreation will be no exception. No, you will not meet my Father as man or woman but as a missing link to the holy circle from whence you came." Sebastein then kissed her on the forehead, gazed at Father Andreas, and said, "Never violate the rules of social interaction by underestimating what a person will or will not do. Always treat the best of friends as a potential enemy."

Monique turned to Father Andreas and asked him if he would like to leave. Father Andreas got down on his knees again in reverence to Sebastein and said farewell. But before he left he asked Sebastein if he could come and visit him, talk to him again, and be there by his side in his last hour.

Sebastein replied, "You have honored the son of man in a way that will bring you all the majestic glory should you enter my Father's kingdom."

They said their farewells and as they walked away from Sebastein, Monique turned and looked at him as he continued to sit in silent meditation.

They continued to walk as Alimar escorted them outside. But before leaving, he asked them to promise not to reveal anything about the master—that the world would know in due time. They gave him their word that nothing would be revealed about Sebastein.

10

On their way back from Sebastein's mansion, Monique and Father Andreas indulged in their individual thoughts. Father Andreas was not yet over his shock. He turned to Monique and said, "The son of God. I have lived to see the son of God. And you, my child, oh how you are blessed. Now I know why you were reluctant to mention what was upsetting you so much. Besides, who would believe us? They would probably lock both of us in an asylum somewhere."

Monique laughed and Father Andreas could not hold it in any longer as he laughed aloud as well.

"You know what is so funny?" asked Father Andreas.

"What, Father?"

"I have one up on the pope." Together they laughed aloud in an unstoppable fashion. A couple minutes later they were very serious once again as their thoughts were filled with Sebastein.

"Think of the things this man has seen, my child. And all that time we here on Earth thought he was in Heaven when in actuality he had come back."

They talked for a while until Father Andreas reached his home. Before leaving the car, he kissed Monique and blessed her. Suddenly a thought hit him and he said to Monique, "My child, you are the one who should be blessing me." They stared at each other for a while, then said their good-byes once again.

Father Andreas and Monique did not see each other until a couple of weeks later, when they met again in Sebastein's garden. They frequently visited Sebastein, talking to him, trying to get to know him better. Monique not so much in a romantic sense, but on a spiritual level, almost on the same level on which Father Andreas was trying to probe and know Sebastein better.

A few more days went by and upon their arrival at Sebastein's mansion, they were told by Sebastein that he would die on the upcoming Friday.

Father Andreas said, "Is this not a strange coincidence that this is Good Friday?"

Sebastein looked at him, then turned to Monique and asked, "Will you give me your hand in marriage on the eve of my death?"

Monique looked at Father Andreas then back at Sebastein. "Gladly."

Over the weeks they had grown very close to Sebastein. They had come to know him not only as Sebastein the man, but as Sebastein the Messiah. They indulged in the privilege of asking and getting answers to their questions, answers that could only have come from the son of God. They were secure in their belief, with no more doubt that Sebastein was, indeed, the Messiah and whatever they decided to do they did gladly.

It was now the eve of Good Friday. In fulfillment of her promise and dressed in a beautiful, white, long gown, Monique walked down the aisle and took Sebastein's hand. He was dressed in a long white robe with a turban around his head, for a moment looking as if he were a sheik of Saudi Arabia. They knelt together at the altar. Father Andreas had provided the church and ensured the secrecy of the event. The congregation was made up of just four people: Alimar, Father Andreas, and two other faithful servants who stood behind the blessed couple in silence as they listened to Sebastein recite words in Latin. Father Andreas felt slighted that he was not asked to perform the ceremony, but then he thought if any man can marry himself, surely it's the Messiah.

As Sebastein spoke, a bright light suddenly came from the cross, which was in front of them on the wall, and Father Andreas's eyes opened wider as if for the very first time since he had known this man who claimed to be the Messiah, he was a hundred percent certain that this was indeed the son of God. The bright light from the cross shined on the couple. Monique was a little scared; but sought comfort in knowing that whatever was happening it had to be good, for it was ordained by God. Within a few minutes the light was gone and Sebastein turned to Monique, kissed her gently on the lips, and said, "It is done." They slowly walked over to Father Andreas, Alimar, and the two servants. Sebastein touched each of them on the shoulder, acknowledging their loyalty.

Father Andreas asked, "I have no doubt that you are the son of God, but why Sebastein as a name and not the name you were born with, the name Jesus?"

"Can you imagine the response that I would get from my people, especially those who have rejected me, if I were to go around calling myself Jesus? They rejected me then, and they would reject me now. Whatever I do for them, I do it in the name of my Father, not to glorify myself. Besides, as a poet once asked, what is in a name?"

Father Andreas said, "I guess you are right. Will the world ever know that you were here, Sebastein?"

"Tomorrow each man will know within his heart that God lives."

Before Father Andreas could ask Sebastein what he meant, Sebastein walked off, saying that he had to be alone. Father Andreas watched him walk off by himself, leaving his bride and his dear friends behind. Somehow they knew within their hearts that they would never see him again.

Alimar took Monique back to Sebastein's mansion, where as part of the prophesy she would live for a year—or longer, if she wished—but she must stay there for at least a year. Though not knowing the reason behind this, she agreed, for she knew that whatever it was, it was good—for Sebastein was good. It took a lot to convince her parents, but she knew what she wanted to do. Although they were not pleased with the idea, they respected her wishes and gave her their blessing, for whatever made her happy was their number one priority.

With or without their blessing she was destined to do what she had to do.

On the morning of Good Friday, the Heavens paid tribute to Sebastein, capturing the attention of all beings that walked the Earth. Many observed the clocks as they wondered why 8:00 A.M. seemed like midnight. People looked outside their windows and stood on their balconies and verandas amazed by the strange figure in the sky. On this morning they were not greeted by the sun, but rather by the moon that had planted itself in the birthplace of the sun. The moon appeared three times its usual size and was accompanied by a bright light in the shape of a cross. The blood dripping from the moon disguised the human-like figure that is usually present. Morning, noon, and night embraced one another for the first time, bringing the world to a standstill, acknowledging once again the death of the Messiah.

It was now 11:00 A.M., a time when the weather in California is usually hot, a time when people would be out on the beach, but it was not like that this day. The darkness was still on the land, and only a handful of people knew what this sign marked—that the son of God had once again laid down his life for humanity. There were reports on the radio, all over the world, of an unusual sign in the sky. People from all nationalities gathered outside their homes, kneeling down as they stared at the sky. All the TV programs were interrupted to bring reports of this unusual occurrence in the sky and the darkness that was sweeping the Earth.

People became more and more alarmed, thinking that the world must be coming to an end when they learned that the entire world was in darkness at the same time. Little did they know that it was once again an opportunity for them to see and to live in such a way that they would do justice to the heavenly Father. It was once again an opportunity to lay down their arms and promote love and peace throughout the world, to honor the death of a man who for centuries had walked among them.

Meanwhile, back at Sebastein's mansion, Monique, Alimar, and Father Andreas kneeled outside as they watched the moon and thought of Sebastein, wherever he might be. The darkness and the unusual-looking moon remained the entire day throughout the world as meteorologists speculated about the cause of this phenomenon. This was a day of reckoning, a day of atonement, a day, Sebastein said, on which the entire world would know that God lives.

Next morning, things were back to normal. Still the topic of discussion throughout the entire world was the strange night, a night that no one would soon forget. People from all over the world gathered in churches by the thousands—people who had never set foot in a church for many years now found themselves in a place of worship.

During this time, while millions of people were gathering in churches, Monique was also getting ready to do the same thing. But before doing so she was making sure she had her breakfast. Monique noticed that she had a very hefty appetite and commented on it to Alimar. "I have never eaten so much before."

"It is understandable, madam. After all, you are eating for two," he said with a big smile on his face.

Monique was surprised by his comment and asked, "What do you mean I am eating for two?"

Alimar became alerted to the fact that he had spoken out of turn and he tried desperately to cover his mistake. "I am sorry, madam, what I meant is that you are eating *as if* you were eating for two people."

"I must say I am, aren't I?"

As Alimar walked away, he closed his eyes for a second or two and sighed, signifying a great relief.

Soon thereafter, Monique was off to church, and at the end of the service Father Andreas approached her and asked her how she was doing. They talked about the sign Sebastein told them the world would see, as they gained reassurance that indeed he must have been the Messiah. Father Andreas asked Monique if she had seen Sebastein or his body, and Monique said no and told him that she sensed that Alimar knew where Sebastein was but refused to tell her or to give her any information, at least not yet. Father Andreas told her that if there was a ceremony to put his body at rest she should be sure to let him know so that he could be a part of it. She promised him she would as she left the church.

That same night as Monique twisted and turned in the bed, missing Sebastein in more ways than one, her inability to sleep was further disturbed by a noise she heard outside her window. She looked outside and saw three men, with torches in their hands, carrying a huge box. She was very concerned. She put her robe on and dashed downstairs after the men. As she got closer, she noticed the men were Alimar and the servants. She was curious about the huge box they were carrying and she watched them as they took the box to a place that seemed to be like a grave, with a headstone that simply said, HERE LIES MY MASTER. HIS DEATH HAS FREED THE ENTIRE WORLD ONCE AGAIN. Monique realized that this was Sebastein's resting place. She came from behind the bushes where she was hiding and the men were surprised to see her.

"Why didn't you tell me?" she asked Alimar angrily.

"We did not think it was necessary to concern you with the details of his death. We have anointed his body and have done what was necessary. Now all that needs to be done is for us to lay his body at rest. We did not tell you because we did not want to trouble you anymore."

"My God, Alimar. He has made me a part of his life. You are not troubling me."

Alimar took her hands and he walked her closer to the coffin. They opened it and they looked at Sebastein, who seemed at peace with himself. Monique thought to herself how at least he was able to die peacefully and was not crucified in such a savage manner. After a few minutes, they closed back the coffin, slowly laid it into the ground, and covered it. No one shed tears. They seemed uplifted by his death, as if they truly understood what it meant for the entire world.

They walked back to the house, and Monique returned to her bed. As she lay there trying to sleep, she burst out in tears as she uttered to herself, "I miss you, Sebastein. I miss you so much."

Weeks later, Monique noticed that she had missed her period and became concerned. Her periods had always been regular and she could time them to the hour. She examined herself carefully. She noticed that her breasts were tender, which could cut both ways, either that her period was still coming or that she was pregnant. She called up her gynecologist and was thankful that she could get an appointment for the next day. The thought of waiting longer to find out for sure would be unbearable.

She sat facing the mirror and thought, *Imagine me trying to tell people that I am carrying the Messiah's child, they would certainly commit me. But then again, how would I raise this child all by myself. Perhaps the whole trauma surrounding Sebastein's revelation that he was the Messiah, our marriage, and then his death might be the reason for the missed period. Stress, that's it. Boy, have I had my share these few days!*

The next day Monique went to her gynecologist, and her suspicions were confirmed that she was pregnant. Monique was elated and very surprised even though it was one of the obvious options she had prepared herself for. Still, she was very concerned. That evening she told Alimar about the news; she told him that she was going to have Sebastein's child. She noticed that Alimar did not seem surprised. Instead, he simply got down on his knees, kissed her feet, and paid his respect to the unborn child as well as to its mother.

"I will take care of you both."

"I know you will, Alimar. I have no doubt that you will."

11

Several months passed and as Monique's pregnancy began to show, her vanity took over. "Look at me," she said to Father Andreas, who was paying her a visit. "I look like a balloon."

"May I ask you a question, my child, without you taking offense?" asked Father Andreas with a concerned look on his face.

"Sure, Father."

"Are you sure it is Sebastein's child?"

Monique was annoyed but did not show it. "As God is our witness, Father, it is Sebastein's child."

"Do you know what this means, my child? For some reason you are carrying the child of Christ and he will continue to play a part in the prophesy."

"I don't know about that, Father. All I know it's my baby and I will do the best for it whether it's a boy or girl."

"I know you will. But you must understand that even Mary had to let go and witness the fate of her son. You must also prepare yourself that a time may come in your life when you will have to let go and allow the child to fulfill its destiny, whatever that may be."

Monique looked at Father Andreas, hugged him, and said, "Please stand by me, Father. I don't think I can do this alone."

"You are not alone, my child. God himself is with you."

Later on that evening, Monique received another visitor. This time it was Paul. "Paul, what are you doing here? How did you know where to find me? I thought I asked Mom and Dad not to tell anyone where I was for the moment."

"Why, Nick told me, of course."

"Nick? I thought he was supposed to be my bodyguard."

"Well, you haven't been using him so we have been finding other work for him in the meantime. Besides, I am the one who made sure he got the job, in case you didn't know."

"Oh, I didn't know that."

Paul was surprised to see that Monique was pregnant. "Well, are you going to invite me in?"

"Sure. Come on in."

As Paul entered Sebastein's mansion, the first thing he did was to comment about the beauty and size of the place. "Sebastein must be a very rich man."

"In more ways than one."

"I take it you two are married now?"

"Yes."

Paul was disappointed with her response because he knew that he had lost all chance of ever being with Monique. For years now he had fantasized about making her his wife. Suave as he was he tried not to display any emotions that would make Monique aware of his disappointment. Rather he walked closer to her and said, "Sebastein is a very lucky man."

Monique could sense that he was really sincere. He was not his usual sarcastic and cynical self. "Thank you, Paul. That's very kind of you."

"So where is the lucky prince?"

"He went on a trip."

"He must be out of his mind to leave you alone by yourself in your state."

"I don't mind. Besides, as you can see I am in no condition to do any travelling."

"Yes, I have noticed. I take it that is why you haven't been coming around to your parents' house?"

"I'd rather not for the moment. You understand, don't you?"

"I guess I do. How long do you intend to keep your pregnancy a secret from them?"

"What makes you think they are not aware of it?"

"Well, being your father's closest friend and attorney, I would have heard something about it by now if they were. Believe me, they are not aware of it."

"That's good, and that's the way I would like it to stay for a while."

"Why? Is something wrong?"

"After the baby is born I will let them know, but right now I can't afford to be going through any mental strain. And you know my parents, especially Dad."

"Yes, I know what you mean."

"Do I have your word that you won't say anything to them."

Paul stared at her for a while, then said, "I know we haven't been the best of friends. But now that you are married and you seem happy I would like to change that. I guess one of the first things to do is to give you my assurance that I won't say anything to your parents. I will do everything in my power to distract them should I get the impression that they are getting close to finding out."

She leaned over, kissed Paul on the cheek, and for the first time the two seemed to share a new and special bond.

"Charlene has been asking for you just about everyday," Paul said, interrupting the temporary silence between them.

"I know I should call her but I don't feel like talking to anybody just yet. Would you please give her my love the next time you see her?"

"Sure thing. Would you mind if I stopped in occasionally, just to check up on you?"

"That would be very nice, and I would really like that."

Paul took her hand, caressed it gently, and said his goodbyes. She walked him to the door and watched him walk out of sight. After Paul left, Monique began to feel tired. She went upstairs to lie down for a while. Soon Alimar and the two other servants, who always seemed to be with Alimar, were by her side in the room, inquiring whether they could do anything to make her feel more comfortable.

"You all have been so good to me."

Alimar looked at her and said, "We are honored to be in your presence, for blessed are you among all women."

Monique realized that they were once again kneeling to her and said, "Please don't do that; please don't kneel to me."

They slowly got up and then went away so she could get her rest.

*   *   *

Time passed, as the months of carrying Sebastein's child took hold on a woman who was told that one day she would bear the fruit of a king. Although her beauty remained intact, she frequently found herself at the mercy of her vanity, thinking how the entity inside her made her feel as if she was about to give birth to the Golden Buddha of Bangkok. She found herself sleeping much more than usual, and this night was no exception.

It was only 9:00 P.M. and already Monique was fast asleep. Before she fell asleep, she had lain awake for hours reminiscing on the days when she would party all night with Charlene and only take a breather in the time it took to shuttle to the next hot spot. A few hours into her deep sleep, she felt the child within her stomach kick so hard; for a moment it was as if Joe Montana had just made a field goal. Being fully conscious, she screamed in pain and in seconds Alimar and the other two servants were by her side. They had moved into the rooms close by in case Monique needed them. After examining her, their suspicions were confirmed. Monique was in labor.

The three ancient physicians cleared the path for what was to be the child of the Messiah. Between contractions, Monique shouted at them, "What are you doing? I have to go to the doctor. I must get to the doctor!"

"No, madam, it is not necessary. We will take care of you. You will be alright. Besides, this is the Master's wish," said Alimar.

Another contraction hit Monique and she screamed, "Get this thing out of me. It's the devil!" She continued to scream in a frenzy. Her breathing was uncontrolled because she had not had the benefit of a Lamaze class. She was sweating profusely. Now she wished she had told her mother or Charlene about the pregnancy because she could have had one of them

108

to comfort her. Monique felt like she was burning up from the sweat and heat. These three old men milling around the room were not helping because it looked like they didn't know what to do. As the contraction eased, she turned her head to the right for a brief respite. She noticed that the servants had stopped dead in their tracks as if mesmerized by something.

"Why are you standing there? Do something! Get this thing out of me!" she yelled. She noticed that they ignored her plea and genuflected as they gazed at the two front posts of her four-poster bed. She slowly followed their eyes to the posts and couldn't believe what she was seeing. She shook her head and closed her eyes, thinking the pain must be causing her to hallucinate. She opened her eyes, but this was no hallucination. The sight was as plain as the nose on her face.

"What the hell is going on?" Monique screamed as she tried to get off the bed.

"Do not be concerned, for it is only a sign that even Lucifer is willing to honor this occasion," Alimar said.

The labor pains gradually subsided as Monique looked at the two cobras wrapped around the bed poles. A dove was sitting on the head of each cobra. The eyes of the snakes were trained on her stomach.

Meanwhile, Alimar checked and saw that the baby was coming. The baby's head slowly emerged from its mother. Alimar took the baby by the head and gently guided the child's delivery into the world. Alimar clipped the umbilical cord and raised the child to the Heavens, and they heard Monique whisper, "My God, look at that. Is it a boy or girl?"

"It's a boy," replied Alimar.

They all watched as the two tiny doves devoured the two ten-foot cobras. "The truce is over," said Alimar as he witnessed the grotesque sight. Alimar placed the child in Monique's arms while she rested and once again he and the servants bowed down to them. This time Monique wasn't as sure whether they were bowing down to her or the newborn child. She was too tired to tell them to stop.

The next morning, Monique called Father Andreas, and although she was still tired from the night's ordeal, she was able to tell him it was a boy. Father Andreas was excited at the great news. In an hour he was at Sebastein's mansion, wanting to see the son of the Messiah. Father Andreas was brought up to Monique's room by one of the servants and as he entered the room and saw the baby in Monique's arms he got down on his knees and bowed to both of them. Being a creature of habit, he attempted to bless the child but suddenly realized that it was not necessary, for this was the son of the Messiah. He stayed with Monique for about two hours and they talked about the labor and the medical skills of the three servants.

On the third day after the child's birth, Alimar and the two other servants called Father Andreas and invited him over to what they told him would be a special ceremony for the baby. He was told to be there at 1:00 P.M.

Meanwhile, upstairs, Monique was still asleep. She turned and got up, looked inside the crib and noticed that her baby was not there. She was startled but sought comfort in the possibility that Alimar or one of the other servants might have taken him. She came to the top of the stairs just in time to see Father Andreas talking to Alimar.

"Monique, my child, how do you feel?" asked Father Andreas.

"As well as can be expected. Alimar, have you seen the baby?"

"Not to worry, madam, he is quite well."

A smile came to her face. "I thought as much," she replied. She suddenly realized that she had not been aware or had forgotten that Father Andreas was supposed to be visiting her that day. "I am sorry, Father, but I am afraid I am not dressed for company. I forgot that you were coming." Father Andreas told her that Alimar had invited him to a special ceremony for the child and that's why he was there.

Monique turned to Alimar. "Ceremony? What ceremony?"

Before Alimar could answer the question, the two servants came, nodding their heads, signifying something of the unknown.

"Who is with my baby?"

Alimar did not answer Monique's question. He went up the stairs, held her by the hand and slowly helped her down.

"What is going on? Where is my baby?"

Alimar still did not answer, just continued to walk with her. They took Father Andreas and Monique to the other end of the mansion, to a room that Monique, even after living there for close to a year, did not know existed. They entered the room. They saw the baby on a small bed and a man standing beside the bed with his back turned. The man was wearing a red robe and Monique noticed that even from the rear he looked very familiar. They all entered the room; Alimar got down on his knees and told them they should kneel also. One of the servants took a chair and allowed Monique to sit.

"What's going on?" Monique continued to ask in a curious manner. "Who is he?" she inquired about the man whose back was turned toward the baby.

Alimar spoke to the man. "Master, we are here." As he said those words, the man slowly turned around.

Monique shouted, "Sebastein, Sebastein." Overcome with joy to see him, she attempted to rush over to him but Alimar held her back and told her that no one could touch him at this moment, for he had to enter his Father's kingdom free from all earthly iniquities and the sins of humanity.

Staring at Monique, Sebastein spoke. "A time will come when our love will know no ends; there will only be beginnings, a life we will share throughout eternity. The whole heavenly staff will bow down before us and pay tribute to the wife of the Messiah. Your time will come, when I will hold you in such a way that will give you pleasure and feelings that will transcend the human senses, for you will be in a world where the ultimate pleasure will be to have touched and been loved by me."

"Sebastein, there are so many things I don't understand."

111

"Woman, seek not to unravel the mystery of the prophesy but to abide by the faith of the heavenly Father who has blessed you with the son of the Messiah." Sebastein then turned to Father Andreas and said to him gently, "You have shown great faith in me and the prophesy. I will set a place at my Father's table for you in hopes that one day you will be a part of his kingdom.

Before long, Sebastein looked at the three servants, revealing their true identities for the first time in two thousand years. "Peter," he said, looking at Alimar, "I called you the Rock two thousand years ago and to this day you have been living up to the name. You have done well. You chose atonement for the mistake of denying me centuries ago. You were forgiven then by the son of man and my heavenly Father, yet you humbled yourself and continued to serve the son of man. Thank you, Peter."

"I will be your disciple forever," replied Peter.

Father Andreas and Monique looked at Alimar, whose true identity was Simon Peter, in amazement and disbelief. Then they looked at the two other servants who were still on their knees, looking at Sebastein.

Sebastein looked at another of the servants, stared at him and said, "Judas, my faithful servant, you betrayed your master with a kiss and were told by the son of man that your action was part of a preordained prophesy. You insisted on making atonement just like Peter. Judas, my faithful servant, you too are blessed among men."

Again a sense of disbelief was in the air as Father Andreas and Monique continued to look in amazement. For so long they had thought of the two men merely as servants, when all along they had been the first followers of Christ. Sebastein stared at the third servant. Monique and Father Andreas looked around in curiosity, wondering who this other man was whom they had been blessed with and had the privilege of knowing.

Sebastein spoke again. "And you, Thomas: you doubted the son of man. You also have felt the need to make atonement like your two brothers, and although you too were forgiven you chose to live a life beside the son of man. For that I am grateful. You three have served me well and are welcome in my Father's kingdom. Yet, you must continue and devote now all the faithfulness and the loyalty to my son that you have shown me, for now it is his time. He must take up my cross and continue the ordeal that will cleanse this entire world of the sins that I have seen."

Sebastein looked at his son and said, "I will call him Elijah after a great prophet of long ago, and he will bring new meaning to the name." Sebastein raised his head up to the heavens and shouted, "Father! Father! I am coming home. But before I do, suffer my son not to see what I have seen, for I have given up the spirit time and time again that he may not have to do so. Smile on him that men may know that when he walks he is my son. Grant him the patience that he will need to understand their follies. Help him, Father, that one day I may say, 'This is my son, with whom I am well pleased.' "

Sebastein then gazed at his audience and said softly, "Until we meet in my Father's kingdom, I will be with you in your thoughts, in your mind and in your soul always." As he said those words, a bright light came from behind him, and within seconds he was almost consumed by the bright light, and then he was nowhere to be found.

Peter went over to the baby, picked him up, and placed him in Monique's arms. She caressed Elijah's cheek. She stared at Peter, Judas, and Thomas, looked at their old frail bodies and wondered how this could be, but knowing that they were part of the prophesy, it had to be.

Father Andreas stared at the three disciples and for the first time bowed to men of God whom he had thought were merely servants. They raised Father Andreas to his feet as Peter said, "We are no better than you. We are merely disciples of God as you are. Please do not bow to us."

Father Andreas looked at Judas and said, "I thought you hung yourself according to the Scriptures and that many of you met your fate at the hands of the Romans. How could this be?"

They looked at each other and said, "With God, all things are possible," as they slowly left the room and went back downstairs, leaving Monique, Father Andreas, and Elijah behind.

12

Monique lay twisting and turning on the fabric where her child, the entity who held the kingdom which was at hand, was conceived. Awakened by the silence that usually binds a mother and a child in times of peril, she got up and noticed that her child was not in his crib. She held her head in despair as an unusual sound rang out from a room close by. Foreseeing the worst, she hurried to the room from where she assumed terror had become the playground for her child. Maternal instinct or just a whim, she did not know. All she knew was that the sound carried with it a sign of caution.

She opened the door and screamed frantically, "What are you doing with my baby?" as she witnessed Peter placing her child in an apparatus shaped like an Egyptian pyramid. The apparatus was made of steel and had an extended arm that looked as if it was a key branch to the body of the mechanical device that was rooted in the ground of destruction. Monique rushed to the aid of her baby, but was stopped by Judas, who placed her in a headlock like a cop trying to restrain a two-hundred-and-fifty pound addict who is withdrawing from heroin. He and Thomas wrestled her to the ground.

Peter looked at the child as its feet and legs moved sporadically in the air and a little grin crossed his face. He leaned over and kissed the child on the forehead, then slowly turned the knob of the apparatus in which the child was placed. Suddenly the aroma of gasoline was in the air.

Realizing what was about to happen, Monique screamed, "Oh, God, no, not my baby!" as she continued to kick and scream, trying to break free of Thomas and Judas, who had her pinned to the ground.

Peter lit the extended part of the apparatus and the entire device was engulfed in flames, while Monique's struggle with the servants intensified. She got one of her feet free and kicked Judas in the face, landing him on a small table, but within a moment time he was on top of her again. Her movements had become so erratic and wild by now that her nightgown was torn and her underwear had found itself at her knees as a result of the struggle. Fatigued from the struggle and realizing that her effort was futile, she took one last look at the flames that were consuming her child and passed out.

A few hours later, she woke up and found herself back in her room, her consciousness clouded and with a slight headache searing across her forehead. She ran her fingers through her hair. Remembering her unthinkable ordeal, she got up and rushed over toward her baby's crib. "Thank God, it was all one bad dream," she said as she picked up the infant, showered him with kisses, then raised him in the air. So engrossed in her joy of being with her child, she didn't notice that Peter, Thomas, and Judas had entered the room.

"Is everything alright?" asked Peter.

"Yes, everything is just fine. Except for a terrible nightmare I had, everything is wonderful."

"Good; we'll be downstairs if you need anything," replied Peter as he and the others left the room. They stopped immediately outside her door and for a second or two stared at each other before leaving her alone.

That night in the same room where Monique assumed her nightmare had taken place, the three men assembled. "The Master's baby has been cleansed by the fire of the Holy Ghost," said Peter. His words brought forth an image of Sebastein who stood before them in silence. "Master, the baptism by fire is completed," said Peter. Those words sent the image of Sebastein disappearing in the same manner in which it had appeared.

13

Longing for a change, Monique and her son went to live in London. It was now eighteen years later and Elijah had bloomed into a handsome young man. Although he was the son of the Messiah, he had enjoyed a relatively normal upbringing. He savored many of the bedside stories Peter told him about prophets and miracles, and how people lived for centuries without dying. By the time Elijah had reached age seven he'd developed an avid interest in books on philosophy, the metaphysical, biblical times, and reincarnation, among other subjects. His readings and his mother's stories about his father generated his interests in travelling. Elijah had travelled extensively throughout the Middle East and Europe, tracing Sebastein's pathways in efforts to learn more about the father he never knew. Now he was settled in a university, beginning his second term of classes.

On the third day of classes, while walking to the library, Elijah ran into Patrick, his best friend. Elijah had been wondering why he had not seen Patrick on the first day of classes because they were in the habit of selecting at least one class together. After the first week of sharing a class with Patrick, Elijah decided to befriend him. He had that calm, quiet disposition like Elijah. Debate was Elijah's forte: long debates. Many of Elijah's classmates got tired after thirty minutes or so, often finding Elijah's views too radical or off the wall. Not Patrick, though. He would engage Elijah in debates for hours and would revel in even the smallest victory.

Elijah saw a distraught look on Patrick's face even though he was trying to appear congenial, as if he was rushing off to an important meeting.

"What's the hurry?" asked Elijah.

"Hi," replied Patrick, almost walking into Elijah. "No hurry, I am just a little busy, that's all."

Elijah knew that this was out of character for Patrick and urged him to go someplace where they could talk. Patrick agreed. Soon thereafter both friends found themselves sitting in Trafalgar Square munching on peanuts.

"So, what gives?" asked Elijah.

"Nothing, let's just forget it," replied Patrick.

"Come on, what's the matter? Simone giving you the blues again?"

Patrick tried to fight back the tears but couldn't. He rested his head on his friend's shoulder and sobbed, "I'm HIV positive; I found out only yesterday."

Elijah was stunned by the news.

Patrick continued sobbing. "How could I have been so stupid and irresponsible?" he said.

"If my father the Messiah could have made a mistake, why not you?"

"Your father? the Christ? Come on Elijah, I know you're weird, but let's get serious. I don't know my Bible very well but I know that Christ was incapable of making any mistakes. He was divine."

"Divinity is not synonymous with perfection."

"What do you mean?

"Having been born the son of God did not preclude him from making errors."

"But I thought being the son of God automatically made him perfect."

"If he was perfect, as you believe, then how could he have made the mistake of selecting Judas for a disciple?"

"I'm not sure I follow you."

"Would you agree that having Judas as a disciple was a mistake—that is, before he found redemption through the grace of atonement?"

"I suppose so," said Patrick reluctantly.

"Then it is safe to say that Christ made a mistake in having him as one of his disciples, is it not?"

"Listen, I don't think I should be having a discussion like this. A man in my position can't afford to be in any more hot water with anybody upstairs."

"It is only through your unwillingness to challenge the obvious will you anger the gods."

"But all my life I have been learning that God or Christ is perfect. Now you are telling me that they are not. Sorry, Elijah, but that's a little bit hard for me to swallow."

"God is the epitome of perfection and has always been so, but Christ was not privileged to the essence of perfection until his resurrection. You see, Patrick, death is the ultimate energizer of life and the epitome of spiritual purging that comes only when the spirit gains liberation from a sinful body. True perfection, the height of one's spirituality, a nirvanic state if you will, can only be attained through death. Remember, my friend, this is not only with Christ, but with anybody."

Realizing that the conversation had taken a more uncomfortable turn for Patrick, Elijah returned to Patrick's concern. "Have you told Simone?"

"How the hell can I?"

"You've got to tell her so she can get tested."

"But why did this have to happen to me? What the hell did I ever do to God to deserve this?"

"I thought you did not believe in the existence of God."

"I don't. Maybe this is his way of getting my attention," replied Patrick as he tried to force a smile through his tears.

"I am sure he would have thought of a better way," replied Elijah as he, too, tried to force a smile.

"Well, what do you think now that you know? Do you still want to be my friend?"

"No! I will always be more than just a friend."

"I am scared, Elijah, scared to die, scared to tell Simone, scared to tell my parents. I am a mental wreck."

"They'll understand, you know that."

"What about Simone? We were thinking of getting married. Do you think she's going to marry me now? We were already having problems. She told me a week ago that although she loves me, sometimes she doesn't think she knows me because of my moods. This virus will only make things worse between us."

"If nothing else, remember that love is constant; once you love a person you will always love that person. Patrick, true love does not come from knowing a person but rather from a spiritual connection that transcends all earthly experiences. Besides, when a romantic experience fails to actualize to its fullest potential, it's only because both souls were meant to travel different paths."

"For someone who is only eighteen you sound like my grandfather."

"You'll be alright; you have to believe you will."

"Hell, I guess we all got to die sometime, right?"

"Life is as transparent as the air we breathe. The tighter you hold onto it, the more likely you are to lose it. You see, Patrick, death is a process that begins at birth. Unless you become one with it, the anticipation of it will be death within itself."

"Maybe I should seriously start thinking about believing in God."

"Each man is the creator of his own God. Maybe you should start believing in yourself and sort out your feelings!"

Elijah and Patrick stared at each other for a while. A few seconds went by before any words passed between the two.

"I have made some mistakes along the way and I am afraid of dying because I don't want to go to hell. It's ridiculous; I don't believe in God but here I am worrying about going to hell."

Elijah did not respond; he just looked at Patrick; a look of empathy.

"I am so confused; I don't even know what I believe in anymore. When they told me I had tested positive, it was as if everything in the universe stopped for a moment. I could not hear or feel anything except my own heartbeat. Do you know what I mean, Elijah?"

"Yes, I do."

Patrick took a deep breath and sighed. He sounded stressed, almost as if he were carrying the entire world on his shoulders. In addition to the support, Elijah tried to give him some reassurance. He did not know how to react to Elijah's comment and the conviction in which it was projected.

"There is no hell in my father's kingdom."

"You say that as if you know for sure."

"I do."

"I've always known you were older than my grandfather," said Patrick jokingly. Patrick realized that Elijah was very serious.

Elijah continued, "There is only oblivion."

"Are you saying that oblivion is an alternative to hell?" Patrick interrupted.

"The alternative to hell as you know it would be heaven."

"I'm not following you, man."

"Torment, hell, morality, are all concepts created by man not only to manipulate our existence but also to restrict our spiritual liberation." Elijah bent and picked up a handful of dust. "The dust by itself is nothing unless it is shaped and molded into something. If I choose not to mold it, then it will remain simply nothingness by virtue of its elements. Our heavenly father created us from this nothingness and should our souls be found unworthy, then we too shall return to the nothingness, hence oblivion. You exist by his will."

"So there is no brimstone and fire?"

"Would your parents get satisfaction from watching you burn in flames of fire because you have broken all or most of the rules that they set in place for you?"

"No way, not even if I committed murder; they love me too much."

"Then what makes you think our Father would stoop to such primitive and morbid acts in order to punish his children? Besides, can you image billions of people screaming and yelling from the flames? I am sure even God would get a thundering headache."

"How do you know so much about these things?"

Elijah was accustomed to this question because he had heard it practically all his life. "I do a lot of reading while you are out partying."

"Hey, womanizing is more like it; see where it got me?"

Both friends got up and started back towards the university. On their way, Elijah told Patrick that he was leaving for Rome the next day and would not see him for a while.

"Are you taking this semester off?"

"Yes!"

"But why?" asked Patrick, missing his friend already.

"To give the world a vacation from sin."

14

Elijah rushed to Rome when he heard that the pope was termi-
nally ill. As he approached the Vatican, he admired the work
of the great sculptor Bernini in the reliefs on both sides of
the pathway leading to St. Peter's Basilica and Michelangelo's
masterpiece. Elijah entered the basilica, wandered around
with the visitors for a brief while, then maneuvered his way
toward the pope's residence, which was heavily guarded.

Elijah boldly walked up to the guards, who were trying to
signal him that he was in the wrong place, and asked to see
the pope. The guards looked him over then laughed heartily at
the thought that Elijah had come to see the pope. After the
guards calmed down, the most senior of the four looked at
Elijah compassionately and told him that the pope was not
seeing anyone and even if he was, Elijah could not just walk off
the street and see him like that. The others resumed laughing.

After pleading his case, the senior guard agreed to help
Elijah by passing on his message to the appropriate officials.
Elijah was told he had to wait in the basilica and someone
would come to get him if his wish was granted.

As Elijah waited in the basilica, he slowly looked around
and saw religious artifacts of all kinds, many embracing the
imagination of man's mind. He closed his eyes as his surroundings triggered a recollection of traumatic experiences dating
back two thousand years. In his thoughts he saw Sebastein
being nailed to the cross as a Roman soldier pierced him with
a spear, laughing as the blood poured from Sebastein's side.
Elijah saw newborn babies strapped to their mothers turned
upside down over a hellish flame, while the Egyptian high
priest looked on and chanted, "Burn, burn."

Images continued to flash in Elijah's mind, conjuring up grotesque pictures from the Holocaust as he attempted to use cognitive distraction in hopes of blocking out the screams of the mothers, fathers, and children who were forced into gas chambers of the different Nazi camps. Perspiration flooded Elijah's face and his face grimaced in pain as he saw images of a twelve-year-old girl strapped to an examining table look with a plea for help from the Nazi doctor, who, though he had sworn to preserve life, injected her with a lethal drug then waited to see how long the drug would take to kill her. The little girl's body jerked in convulsion as the Nazi physician checked his watch periodically and uttered, "Die, die."

Elijah's body trembled in a feverish fashion as images of the past continued to consume his mind. A loud noise rang out in his head as he observed the cranium of John F. Kennedy blown to pieces and the body of Martin Luther King fall to the ground. "Father! The mirror of the world seldom reflects the colors of the rainbow," he said, shivering in cold sweat.

By this time visitors to the basilica were curiously watching Elijah from a distance, wishing that someone would help the young man, but no one would go forward, fearing that whatever possessed him might find its way into their body. Realizing that he was the center of attention, Elijah quickly composed himself so that there would be no further alarm. The guards came back and told Elijah that under no circumstances could he see the pope. Elijah turned and walked away.

Meanwhile, the pope lay writhing from pain. Only seconds ago he had ordered everyone out his room. The Vatican staff remained huddled outside his door. Doctors had tried everything but nothing would ease the pope's pain. A sharp pain seared through his body; he cried out in a whisper, "My Lord! please help me; take me if you will." As he said those words, he was shocked when he turned and saw a young man standing by his bed. Although in pain, the shock of seeing this stranger gave the pope momentary strength to pull himself up and ask, "What are you doing here?" as he touched the button beneath his pillow in hopes that his brethren would come to his aid. He saw a gentleness within the young man's eyes and somehow became calmer, as if he had nothing to fear. He then asked, "How did you get past the guards, young man?" But the young man did not answer.

After a while the young man said, "I have come to talk about blessings and absolutions for sins."

Just then the staff rushed into the room, coming to the pope's aid. They surrounded the young man and held his arms. The pope told them to let him go because he wanted to talk to him.

"You have come for my blessing even though I am dying?" asked the pope.

"I have not come to receive your blessing but to give you absolution from your sins and blessings from my father."

"Young man, I have terminal cancer, as you may have heard in the media. My time is near. God is awaiting my presence. There is nothing you or anyone else can do. The doctors tried everything. When your number comes up, there is nothing anyone can do."

"How old are you?" asked Elijah.

"Sixty-three."

"Then you have lived almost half of your life span. Why then do you attribute your death to the will of my Father?"

"Because only God has the power to give and take life away."

"A child runs across the street and is hit by an oncoming vehicle; a woman is brutally slain on her way home from work; a man dies after five years of struggle with AIDS; a priest commits suicide after battling years of depression; should these deaths be considered preordained by God?"

"Indeed, whether we live or die depends on God. When we die it is only because God has some greater plan for us."

"To embrace such beliefs, one needs to ask why God allows us to be born if he has the insatiable desire of snatching us from this Earth during varied stages of our lives."

The pope looked baffled and pensive as he searched for an explanation to Elijah's remark. "It is not for us to question what God does or does not do, young man."

"But it is, for only by doing so will man learn how to separate truth from fiction. When will humanity understand that man ceased to live beyond hundreds of years only because of his deeds? Still, through God's mercy each man is able to live to be 150 years old."

"I have never heard anyone living to be 150 years in this day and age."

"Each man was meant to do just that, for when a child, a man, or a woman dies, the responsibility for the death rests solely on the individual or the circumstances. God does not and will not intervene in deciding who lives and who dies at a particular age, for to do so would interfere with the cornerstone of mankind's salvation."

"And what is that?"

"Free will, the ability to choose our own path, make our own decisions and our own mistakes."

"If what you are saying is true, young man, then I still have over eighty years left to my life. But here I am dying."

"Not by God's will, but because of the law of circumstances."

"Is it not true that God controls these circumstances?"

"Once he did, but he gave the law of circumstances full autonomy over itself when mankind chose the path to free will."

The pope and the Vatican staff were impressed by the young man's words.

"So, you do not believe that God controls these circumstances and that each man's destiny is preordained?"

"The concept of predestination by birth is a myth. A man's entire life is not written in some elaborate book authored by God where the turning of each page becomes the prerequisite for the stages of his life."

"If the concept of predestination does not exist, tell me, young man, what does?"

"I said the concept of predestination by birth does not exist, but what does is predestination by fate."

"And how do you characterize this predestination by fate?"

"Fate is the offspring of the laws of circumstances. Each man's life is governed by these unknown circumstances."

"Should this be the case, then, it would seem that we have no control over what happens in our lives and that God has turned us over to a set of unknown variables. Life would be so futile if this were the case."

"Futility is the shadow of faith and the mold of which endurance for greatness is measured. It is hope ceasing to exist in a time when it is needed most."

"You've lost me, young man. What do you mean by futility is the shadow of faith?"

"You said if our lives were only governed by unknown variables then existence would be futile. But if this feeling of futility, helplessness, and hopelessness was not a part of your psyche, there would be no need for faith."

"So you believe our faith in God is strengthened by this sense of helplessness?"

"It is one of the many units by which it is measured."

"If our lives are governed by a set of unknown variables which you ascribe as the laws of circumstances, knowing that these laws have full autonomy over our existence, how are we suppose to protect ourselves?"

"By becoming in sync with them."

"In sync? In what way?"

"You cannot become one with them unless you have mastered the ability to rally the laws of circumstances in a sequence that will put forth your life in a universal order."

"How can this be done when each variable is so unpredictable?"

"The fact that they are so unpredictable is what makes them predictable."

"So you believe that the laws of circumstances occur at random and sporadically?"

"Yes!"

"If it comes at random, how can you prepare your life or acquire any form of order?"

"Because it comes and that makes it predictable."

"You mentioned rallying these circumstances which in turn would give our lives some meaning. How can one rally a set of unknown events that comes at will, in no timely fashion, and remain in control of one's existence?"

"Pretend for a moment that you're a general in an army, with one hundred men under your command. You, like the laws of circumstances, have the power to place them in any random situation or predicament that you deem necessary. Still, to prevent you from treating them unfairly, they can rally together and compel you to make certain eventful changes that would not be a threat to their lives. So can you with the laws of circumstances. Rally them; become in sync with them in order to shape and make your existence a meaningful one."

The pope listened to Elijah attentively, with a slight smile on his face, then he commented, "I never thought man's relationship with God was so complex and that he would abandon us to a bunch of circumstances."

Elijah sensed the pope was being cynical and responded with sarcasm, "The essence of man's relationship with God is a spiritual paradox. The more knowledge God gives man, the less he thinks he needs God and the more ungrateful he becomes. The spiritual and metaphysical link which should be stronger becomes weaker. Why then should not our heavenly Father blink?"

"Yet he continues to give us wisdom beyond our comprehension!"

Elijah smiled and responded, "Yes, an irony with the premise of the ultimate form of unconditional love."

"By the way, who are you to give me absolution?"

Elijah said in a very firm and direct manner, "I am the son of the Messiah."

His words created a great stir among the Vatican staff who had gathered around him. One accused him of sacrilege and another said they should throw him out for his blasphemous remark against the heavenly Father. Although the pope was shocked by the young man's remark, he waved his hand and the entire room was silent. He looked closer at the young man who stood there in washed-out jeans and sandals, but was even more amazed that this young man who claimed to be the son of the Messiah was far from being white. "Come closer, young man," said the pope. The young man walked closer as the pope asked, "What is your name?"

"Elijah."

"Do you realize the significance of your words? As you may very well know, Christ was divine, and he never had a son. The Christ we know was not a man of the flesh. Although he lived among us, his heart was with God and nothing else."

"Old man, you study the Scriptures but you fail to understand the words of my father."

The room was once again very alarmed by the abruptness and what some of the members considered to be rudeness on the part of Elijah. They begged his holiness to allow them to throw the young man out, but still the pope found him very intriguing and fascinating, to say the least. Once again the pope signaled them to allow Elijah to speak.

"Overcome by your own idiosyncracies and inhibitions, you have blinded yourself to the true image of my father. How can a man who represents the epitome of love fall short to the flesh? Is not our body an instrument of love? Yet you hide yourself behind your puritanic ways, afraid to face what was and what is."

"Young man, you must be about seventeen years old. If you were the son of the Messiah, that would mean that Jesus fathered you roughly eighteen years ago. Am I not right, brethren?"

They all laughed and said, "Yes you are, your holiness."

Elijah was serious and as they laughed he stood there in silence. Then when the room was once again calm, he looked at the pope and said, "But you are almost right."

The pope did not quite understand this comment and asked, "Almost right about what?"

"The son of man left Earth no more than eighteen years ago, fulfilling the true ascension into the heavens according to the prophesy."

This comment infuriated Father Andropolus to the point where he had to speak up. "Must we listen to this, your holiness? This lad is quite mad. Must we listen to him? He speaks so wrong against the son of our heavenly Father."

The pope said, "I am quite amused by this young man. Let's hear him out."

Before the pope could finish his sentence, Elijah attempted to leave, but the pope asked him if he would stay for a while. Elijah stopped and looked at them one by one, dressed in their garments made of the finest cloth. Then he said angrily for the very first time, "Oh Pharisees of the twentieth century, you have seen and heard the son of the Messiah, now you must choose, for I cannot choose for you."

The pope suddenly held his chest, as if he was exhausted from the conversation with Elijah. The Vatican staff rushed over to his bed as he assured them that he was quite alright. Elijah walked over to the pope's bedside, actually shoving his way through.

He looked at the pope, took his hand, and said once again, "Show the world that you are worthy of your position. Accept the son of the Messiah and by tomorrow morning you will be down on your knees giving thanks to the son of man. For by accepting me, you do not dishonor my father but pay tribute to him in the highest form. He came to you two thousand years ago, the son of a carpenter, born in a stable, and you rejected him. Today I come to you as a Black man wearing garments that are not suitable for a pauper's son. Will you reject me, too?" They all noticed Elijah's appearance as if for the first time, pitying him, not knowing of his great wealth.

Elijah's words sent chills up the pope's spine. For the first time the entire Vatican staff started to see Elijah in a different light and started to take him much more seriously, for his analogy was so vivid in their minds. For a moment or two they experienced doubt and this was somewhat scary to them.

The pope looked at his staff and he said to them, "Brothers, pray for me, for maybe for what I am about to do my soul will be forever damned. There is something about this young man that tells me that his heart is true."

The entire room became alarmed and noisy once again. Then the pope raised his hand and the room was once again in silence. He looked at Elijah and said, "Young man, I accept you as the son of the Messiah and if you are ill or under the delusion that you are the son of Christ, may God forgive me and have mercy on you."

Elijah took the pope's hand and said, "Old man, your faith in me has cleansed you from all your sins and your body is once again free from all the earthly afflictions that time has cast on it."

The pope suddenly felt a warmth rushing through his body and he knew from that feeling that he was getting much stronger. The man who had laid there for months waiting to die got off the bed and developed an appetite that surprised even himself. The Vatican staff was astonished. They attempted to hold the pope but he signaled them with his hand, telling them that it was not necessary. They did not want to believe what they were witnessing. The pope got down on his knees and paid tribute to Elijah.

Elijah raised the pope by the shoulders and said, "Your faith has made you whole. Give me not the glory, for whatever I do, I do in the name of my Father."

A few hours later, the pope was paid a visit by his personal physician, at the request of the Vatican staff. The doctor examined the pope, took a few blood samples, and left with a promise that he would return the results of the test as soon as possible. Soon after, based on his examination, the doctor told the Pope that by some strange miracle, he was again as healthy as any man his age could be. Somehow the pope knew that would be the result.

Meanwhile, Elijah was being interrogated by Vatican staff who thought of him not as the son of the Messiah but perhaps as a new Antichrist who came in the body of a child to deceive them.

"Are you the devil?" asked Father Andropolus.

"How ready you are to accept that I am the devil rather than the son of the Messiah. In a world where there is murder by the second, where one of every five movies is made about the ways of Lucifer, paying tribute to him in his highest form, a world where the Ten Commandments are forsaken by man, a world where a man like you sits in judgement of people who are only the victim of circumstances—yes, in a world where billions are spent on arms awaiting the destruction of nations while millions go hungry—the son of the Messiah does not need to pay any more honor to Lucifer. For the world in which you live is the ultimate personification of everything God despises and Lucifer worships."

"We know the world is far from being perfect. But who are you to criticize and question God's wishes?" replied Father Andropolus.

"If all these things were our heavenly Father's wishes then why would my father lay down his life on Calvary? Certainly not for an already perfect world."

"We do not question God's will, young man," replied Father Andropolus.

"Maybe you should, for by doing so you would see that the things you claim to be his will are not but the will of man, a will imposed on man by man in order to control man. This concept you know as secular religion."

"If you were truly religious, you would not stand there and talk such rubbish."

"But I am not."

"You can say that again."

"For there is too much religion and not enough spirituality amongst you worshippers," said Elijah, sarcastically.

"May God forgive you but not forget what you have said here today."

"Old man, forgiving without forgetting is not forgiveness; rather, a hypocritical gesture to prolong hatred."

His words once again created a stir amongst the Vatican staff as they were interrupted by the pope, who walked in the midst of them and slowly rested his hands on Elijah's shoulder.

He looked at Elijah once again in amazement and said, "Whoever you are, you must certainly be the child of God, for it has been confirmed that I have been restored to health one hundred percent."

The Vatican staff was once again alarmed, asking among themselves how could this be and speculating that even if it were, it was the work of the devil. The pope raised his hand and the room became silent. He turned to his staff and said, "I know it is hard to believe, but you can see for yourself I have been made whole by this young man who speaks of God maybe in an unorthodox way, but nevertheless not of the devil but of God. I therefore believe in this young man and his words."

He then took Elijah and slowly walked away, as the Vatican staff walked behind, still in doubt as to the true reason why Elijah was there. The pope, already cleansed with a spiritual metamorphosis that transcends the human eyes, knew within his heart what he had to do. Still, the resolution to his dilemma was far from over, for he saw in the eyes of his counsels—those cardinals, apostolic nuncios, and archbishops from various dioceses—the soul of doubting Thomas, which had become the very essence of their intellectual repertoire.

The pope thought to himself how for the first time the idea of being an agnostic was quite edifying. But the holy light of the almighty God appeared to have stirred his blood, casting a shadow even on neutrality, compelling him to embrace the role he was meant to play in Elijah's destiny. He spoke, announcing his intent, an intent that would launch a conspiracy behind closed doors. "The day after tomorrow I will announce to the world that the son of the Messiah lives."

15

The cardinals grew concerned, for they could see that the clean bill of health the doctor had issued made the pope a believer in Elijah. That same night, four of the Pope's counsels, Father Andrew, Father Andropolus, Father Francis, and Father Antonio, all met in a secret place to discuss the fate of a "possessed pope," as they described him. They sat around a table as Father Andropolus, who appeared to be chairing the meeting, said, "You all know why we are here: to do whatever it takes to put an end to this madness."

"Forgive me, Father Andropolus, but is it possible that this young man could very well be whom he says he is?" asked Father Andrew.

"Dear God, not you, too," replied Father Andropolus.

"I am merely suggesting that we open our minds to all possibilities," said Father Andrew.

"If the pope announces Elijah as the son of the Messiah, the entire world will lose respect for the authority of our positions," interjected Father Francis.

"I agree," commented Father Antonio.

"You know how he gets when he thinks he's right. I have seen him like this on many occasions, and I know he will follow through with telling the world that Elijah is the son of the Messiah. When he is like this, nothing can change his mind, even if it kills him," said Father Andrew. The three men stared at Father Andrew, then their eyes shifted back and forth to one another.

Father Andrew thought for a second, then instantaneously became very alarmed when he noticed that his comrades' facial expressions had changed, and looked as if they had just found a pot of gold. "You can't be serious!"

"Why not?" asked Father Andropolus.

"Why not? Because it goes against everything we stand for," replied Father Andrew.

"Better one man to die physically, than a whole nation of people spiritually," said Father Andropolus.

"Where have I heard that argument before?" asked Father Andrew sarcastically.

"I know someone who can do it," said Father Antonio in a squeaky, childlike voice. The others were surprised that a man whom they had viewed until now as one of the humblest of them all would know someone who would kill for money.

"You, Father Antonio, know of such an individual?" asked Father Francis.

"Yes, I have had need for this individual's service on quite a few occasions. You see, my brothers, in this world it is good to know three types of people: the wealthy, who can buy your way out of any predicament; the loyal, who will blindly lay down their lives for you; and the ruthless, who will gladly kill for you—often for a price, of course." Father Antonio's colleagues were shocked by his comments.

"I am totally against this," said Father Andrew, waving his hand above his head.

"We gather that, but you will support us in these times of trials?" asked Father Andropolus.

"I suppose I have no choice," replied Father Andrew.

"Then it is settled. Father Antonio will contact his associate and make the necessary arrangements. It must be done by tomorrow night the latest. It is imperative that the pope doesn't get the opportunity to address the congregation of St. Peter's Square on Sunday. I know that is when he plans to proclaim that young devil the son of the Messiah. Everything is now in your hands, Father Antonio. Spare no cost, and may God grant us the instrument of our delivery," said Father Andropolus.

The following evening at about 5:00 P.M., Father Antonio requested a meeting with the three co-conspirators, only this time they had a guest. The guest was wearing a traditional Vatican robe, and the person's head was covered with the hood of the robe. In the darkness of the room, the six-feet two-inch giant kept twitching. The face of this unknown giant was as white as the teeth that seemed to be hanging out of the guest's mouth, looking like an orthodontist's nightmare, from between which strange, whispered curses and recriminations would occasionally emerge. Before Father Antonio could introduce the stranger, Father Andropolus called him to the side and whispered, "Is that him?"

"Yes, but there is something you need to know," said Father Antonio, who had been interrupted.

"Why is he twitching like that? Look at him; his head is doing strange things on his body," interjected Father Andropolus. Shortly, they were joined by Father Francis and Father Andrew in a huddle.

"That man just called us hypocrites twice," said Father Andrew angrily.

"Yes, maybe he is not the right man for the job. Who is he to judge us?" asked Father Francis.

"He talks as if he has the hiccups, and that annoying twitching of his. . . . Where did you get him from?" asked Father Francis as he turned to Father Antonio.

"I am sorry, I guess we should have taken out an ad saying 'need killer for the Vatican, send résumé,'" said Father Antonio.

"We are not criticizing you, Father Antonio; we are just concerned as to whether or not he can do the job," said Father Andropolus.

"That will not be a problem. Come, let me introduce you," said Father Antonio. They walked over to be formally introduced. "Brothers, meet—" Before Father Antonio could finish the introduction, the stranger removed the hood. Face to face with a giant albino, the three men looked as if they were about to jump out of their robes.

"Mother of mercy! It's a woman!" said Father Andropolus. Father Francis and Father Andrew were speechless, hypnotized by the physical appearance of the woman.

"Brothers, this is Takita. Takita meet—" Before Father Antonio could finish, he was pulled aside by his three brethren.

"Good lord, have you lost your mind?" asked Father Andropolus.

"And I wish she would stop calling us hypocrites right to our faces," interjected Father Francis.

"She means no disrespect, Father Francis; she has Tourette's syndrome. An impulse disorder, you see," replied Father Antonio.

"Tourette's syndrome? I've heard about that. Yes, now I remember. A mental disorder of some kind," said Father Andropolus.

"Great, not only did he get us a woman, he got us a killer who is already crazy," said Father Andrew.

"She is not crazy," replied Father Antonio firmly.

"She will probably take the knife to us when she is through with the pope," said Father Andrew.

"Nonsense, and who said anything about a knife?" replied Father Antonio.

"Father Antonio is right; the pope's death must look like an accident or as if he died from natural causes," said Father Andropolus.

"What are we going to do?" asked Father Andrew.

"If Father Antonio thinks she can do the job, then we must trust his judgment. Come, we have kept our guest waiting long enough," said Father Andropolus.

They gave Takita the impression that she had their full support and confidence, not knowing that when she called them hypocrites, she did so consciously and not due to a symptomatic idiosyncrasy stemming from her disorder. She knew that Father Antonio, in his usual way, would provide a rationale for her behavior. Besides, who would believe that she had an IQ over two hundred. She listened to them as they mapped out in detail how, where, and when the deed would be carried out.

Two hours later, when they were through filling Takita's head with information, they each hugged her. "Good luck, my child. God be with you," they said one by one.

"Hypocrites," said Takita as she watched them slowly leaving the room. They stopped, turned around, and looked at her without saying a word, then they continued on their way. A big smile came on Takita's face, knowing once again she was able to get away with it.

16

Later that same night, as the Pope and Elijah dined in private, they talked about the Scriptures and the betterment of mankind. Elijah asked the pope if he could see the crucifix the pope was wearing around his neck. The pope paused for a while, then removed the crucifix and handed it to Elijah.

"You may keep it," said the pope.

"Thank you, but only on the condition that it is an exchange," replied Elijah as he went inside his shirt, removed the hidden crucifix from around his neck, and handed it to the pope.

"This is beautiful, Elijah. I have never seen one like this before."

"It would mean a great deal to me if you would keep it. It is nearly two thousand years old, a legacy from my father."

"Are you sure?"

"Yes."

They placed the crucifixes around their necks as they held each other's hands and squeezed softly. Moments later, Elijah said good-night to the pope, allowing him the opportunity to get ready for bed.

Realizing that he was not as sleepy as he thought, the pope took his usual walk. Half an hour later, he returned to his bedroom to prepare for his night's rest. He knelt in front of the crucifix on the wall and began to pray. When he was through praying, he got up and turned down the covers of the bed. He sat down on one side of the bed, sighed, then attempted to lie down when he remembered that he had not read his Bible. He went into another room, where he had left his Bible earlier, and picked it up. On his way back to his bedroom, he looked at his new crucifix hanging around his neck. He kissed it, then opened his Bible as he continued to walk toward his bed. He turned off the overhead light, leaving his entire bedroom in darkness for a moment. Walking like a blind man toward his reading lamp at the side of the bed, he heard a noise behind him. He turned around quickly.

"Who is there?" the pope asked as he walked back to switch on the overhead light. He turned on the light, looked around briefly, saw no one, then attempted the same ritual to get to his bed again. This time he got to his reading lamp. He sat on the side of the bed, not realizing that the sheets he had pulled down were back in place as before. He shook his head as he removed his slippers by using one foot to assist the other. "I don't care what Elijah said. I am getting old; my hearing is not what it used to be," the pope muttered to himself.

He felt a movement on the bed beside him, then slowly turned his head to confirm his suspicions. His awareness was also alerted to the fact that his pillows were not where they were supposed to be. He felt a lump in his bed and kept feeling, trying to ascertain what was under the covers. He felt what appeared to be two feet, and became quite alarmed as he continued his spot check. Convinced that a body was beneath his sheets, he slowly removed the covers. He leapt off his bed as he uncovered the face of Takita.

She swiftly got from under the covers and stood up facing the pope without saying a word. The pope was petrified to see her as she stood before him completely naked. His fear was intensified as he stared at her genital region, noticing that she had a penis in addition to a vagina. He was not sure whether or not he was frightened by the appearance of this albino hermaphrodite who stood before him totally naked or at the peril he sensed was at hand. Takita slowly began to walk toward him, one foot in front of the other, perfectly contained, as if she were a model who had just graduated from a finishing school.

The pope retreated, knocking over a vase on a nearby nightstand. Suddenly pain shot up his left arm. He grabbed the left side of his chest. He stumbled to the floor as Takita watched him struggling to breathe. Realizing that he was having a heart attack, the pope, showing little concern for his own life, crawled to reach the broken crucifix that had fallen from his neck to the floor when he stumbled. Takita looked on. The pope grabbed the crucifix, turned over on his back and tried to alleviate the pain that still pierced through his chest by gripping the crucifix tightly with both hands. His eyes were almost closed, but he was able to see Takita standing with both legs over his body. His vision was blurred, but he was still able to see Takita's penis hanging down while her head twitched involuntarily.

A smile came on Takita's face as she watched his grip loosen, displaying the crucifix on his chest. She leaned over to pick up the crucifix, but before she could a ball of fire ejected from it, sending Takita all the way across to the other side of the room. Taking a life form of its own, the crucifix illuminated a light around the pope's body, bringing him to a point where he was awakened from his unconsciousness. He tried to get up but still felt weak from his ordeal. He felt a helping hand on his shoulder and seemed startled.

"It's alright," said Elijah.

"Elijah, thank God. There was a woman of some sort."

"It's okay, I know," said Elijah as they both walked across the room to look at Takita. The pope turned his head away, unable to look at the grotesque sight of Takita, who lay there with her chest totally demolished by a large burn that was shaped in the form of a crucifix.

"Who is she and how did she get inside here?" asked the pope.

"One of the many demons who would rather not see the prophesy be fulfilled."

Elijah took the pope to another room, where he sat with him until the Pope was calm enough to sleep. As soon as the pope fell asleep, Elijah returned to the pope's bedroom. Looking at Takita he said, "An empty vessel should not be allowed to pay tribute to an empty soul; away from my sight!" He closed his eyes for a second, and when he opened them, Takita's body had vanished into thin air.

17

The next morning, as the pope prepared to address the nations and to reassure them that he was healed, indicating that God lives amongst us, he saw Elijah's reflection in the mirror behind him. He turned, looked at Elijah, and asked, "How did you get in? I did not hear you."

Elijah did not respond. Rather, he stood there in silence, staring at the pope.

"Did you find out who that woman was? What has become of her body? I know she was dead but her body was not where we left it last night."

"Do not be concerned. I have taken care of everything."

"Who was she? What do you mean you have taken care of everything?"

"She was a demon sent by your peers to stop the prophesy."

"You mean she was an assassin?"

"Yes."

"Do you mean to tell me that a plot was devised by my brethren, men of God, to take my life?"

"Yes, but only a handful of men whose eyes are still glued to the darkness of ignorance."

The pope made a fist and hammered away at his knees. "My God! What transgression have I committed to deserve this?" Elijah went closer and rested his hand on the pope's shoulder. "I give you my word, no harm will come to you except the one you bring to yourself. Be strong, for our Heavenly Father could not have chosen a more worthy general. Whom will you say has restored you back to health?"

The pope was quiet and unsure how to answer the question. "I will say a child who has been blessed by God, for no one would believe that Christ had a son."

"Although your words mean well and your heart is sincere, you speak only half the truth. But to fulfill the prophesy you must announce me to the world as the son of the Messiah."

"I have no doubt that you are whom you proclaim yourself to be, young man. But can you imagine the impact on the world if I were to announce that there lives amongst us the son of the Messiah? It would destroy all our teachings, everything people have come to believe in. Nothing would remain as we have known it to be. There would be so many unanswered questions that people would be in a state of panic and confusion, not knowing where to turn. The population of people that have depended on the Catholic doctrine for years would now see us as nothing but a bunch of madmen undecided about the Scripture. They certainly would not believe that you are sane because everything that you stand for is against the Scriptures as we have known them to be."

"Without the prophesy there can be no Scriptures, for the prophesy is the only means through which the Scriptures can be validated."

"What do you mean by that?"

"The Scripture was fulfilled because my father followed through with the prophesy. If it must stay that way, so must I fulfill the prophesy, for without the prophesy the Scripture will die a slow death—as is evident by the things we are witnessing in the world today, things that are against God and the heavenly hosts."

"Surely you must understand the ramifications your presence will have on the world."

"It is for that very reason that the world should know of my presence."

"What you are asking of me would take a long time; it would mean approval from the other cardinals and countless debate."

"You already have the approval; it comes from the most high."

"If I should do as you ask, I am sure that my brothers will declare me mad and do everything in their power to disrupt my service as pope. Are you aware of this?"

"Have you forgotten your Scriptures? Blessed are those who are persecuted for righteousness' sake, for theirs is the kingdom of heaven. They have already tried to kill you. What else can they do?"

"I imagine try to be successful next time!"

"Believe in your heart and your faith will be the light of your reason. Do what you know must be done in order that the prophesy might be fulfilled."

"What is this prophesy you speak of, Elijah? And what is the purpose?"

"Do you believe the Scripture in its entirety?"

The pope seemed puzzled by this question. "I believe. . . ."

"Why do you struggle so hard to find the answer to a question that is so obvious?"

"Yes, young man, I believe in every word of the Scripture," said the pope in such a manner as if he were still trying to convince himself of his belief.

"Then you, too, are in the dark and this is why the prophesy must be fulfilled. The prophesy which I speak of will bring man and God closer again by drawing their attention from the myths and the discrepancies that have become a profound part of the Scriptures throughout translation upon translation. Have you not noticed the contradictions and inconsistencies within the Scripture, which have become so embedded in those who have the faith and have kept it all the time?"

"Is this not the reason why they need people like us to guide them?"

"A blind shepherd cannot lead his flock, much less protect his sheep from falling over a cliff."

"Today I will be the most unpopular man on Earth."

"Count your blessings, for you will be amongst good company."

"Many will not believe. You know that, don't you?"

"Many will and those who do not cannot say that they have not witnessed and seen the Godsend."

"What about the Second Coming; is this still to be?"

"You have heard but you have not understood, for the prophesy represents the Second Coming," said Elijah as he walked away.

The pope sat looking at himself in the mirror, as he seemed somewhat distraught by the conversation he had with Elijah. He tried desperately to wipe the sweat that dripped from his face, ruining it for the camera and his public appearance.

On his way to address his congregation, the pope, walking with Elijah, saw the conspirators in the hallway. When they saw the pope, they looked as if they had seen a ghost. They had planned to take their respective places and await the pope's arrival for mass. Then, when he failed to show, they would pretend to search for him, find his body, and then announce to the world that he had died overnight. This was not the case, however, and they stared at each other in disbelief and utter disappointment. Elijah and the pope could see the guilt on their faces. Without saying a word to them, the pope and Elijah slowly continued to walk, as they fell into line behind.

A short while later the pope was facing thousands of people and millions on worldwide TV. He stared at his speech and for a moment could not find the words as his audience, both live and non-live, wondered what he was doing trying to make a speech after he had been so ill for months from terminal cancer. They did not yet know of his recovery.

Suddenly he found the courage and the strength within himself and said, "I was touched by the heavens and was healed from the crown of my head to the soles of my feet. Yes, my brethren, I am cured of this cancerous disease that has tried to get the best of me. I no longer have cancer, as my doctors have confirmed. I am rid of this affliction through the grace of God." As the pope spoke, in his voice you could sense a tremor that cast a doubt to the audience as to whether or not he was truly healed.

Toward the end of his speech, he said, "My brothers, do not think ill of me for what I am about to say, but I have met and I have seen, and have believed a young man who has claimed to be the son of the Messiah." His words sent his live audience into a frenzy, and the millions of people watching thought they had misheard what he had said. They were confused.

Then the pope reiterated what he had said, "I was healed by the son of the Messiah. Although many people will doubt, this actually happened. Make no mistake about it that I, the pope, was healed, was touched, and was blessed by the son of the Messiah, who walks amongst us as his father did two thousand years ago—or should I say, now that the prophesy has been revealed to me, just a few years ago."

The pope's speech was translated into different languages so that people throughout the world could hear of the coming of the prophesy that was with the son of the Messiah. The entire world was suddenly on fire as neighbors began calling one another, and people from all over the world began to call relatives. The political scenery was like a wildfire. People were conversing over the Vatican telephone lines, which were extremely busy. It was a marked time for what was supposed to be a new beginning, one that entails peace and calm on earth. Still, the pope's speech sent a lot of people into a panicky situation. Some believed it was the end of the world while others thought it was indeed a new beginning. The perception of the world was now viewed by many in accordance with their own deeds, but the one familiar question that seemed to be on everyone's mind was merely whether or not the pope had simply gone mad. Throughout the world, there were mixed emotions about what the pope had said in his speech. People on the buses, husbands and wives, kids in the classroom, all through the world people were discussing the pope's speech the next morning.

Meanwhile, back at the Vatican, the Vatican staff was outraged. They called an administrative meeting along with a couple of psychiatrists and insisted that the pope be thoroughly examined. Father Andropolus even suggested doing an exorcism, thinking the pope was possessed by a demon sent by the devil. They were gathered around the pope's chair, accusing him blatantly of being possessed and being totally reckless in his speech, with no regard for his counsels.

The pope sat and listened to the criticisms and saw their hostility directed towards him, but didn't say anything. He thought how for the first time he was witnessing turmoil and disrespect from a staff that had worshipped with him, prayed with him, and always been there for him, even when he was dying.

His thoughts were broken by the harsh words of Father Andropolus. "You have sold your soul to the devil. In return for health you have condemned your soul to eternal flame."

Before the pope could answer, the sound of Elijah's voice could be heard echoing from behind the staff. "He might touch the face of God, sup with the son of man, and dance with the angels in celebration of this day before any of you are deemed worthy to crawl your way into the kingdom of Heaven."

The staff turned to see Elijah behind them. And in response, Father Andropolus said to him, "You must be the Antichrist; you have come to deceive man, but not me. You will not deceive me."

"Old man, you have already been deceived by your own inability to see beyond your own limitations," said Elijah as he slowly walked among them, making his way to the pope, who looked quite pale by now.

Elijah held the pope's hand and said gently, "Blessed are you amongst men, for you have shown that not only can you lead amongst your people, but because of your faith in me you may have secured your place amongst the highest rank in my Father's kingdom. I came to say good-bye."

"I was wondering where you were."

"Like you, I too find strength in solitude."

"I guess you know what I have been going through."

"Yes. It will pass."

"Will it?" asked the pope, already regretting his actions.

"Soon you will be in their favor once again, and when you are, remember what I am about to say: Here the prophesy begins and here will it end." Elijah kissed the pope's hands, said farewell, then walked away.

18

When Elijah returned home to London, Monique ran and hugged him before he was fully inside the house. "Oh, Elijah, thank God you are safe. Let me look at you, my son. It's funny how a couple days can seem like a lifetime when you are away from the one you love."

"I missed you, too, mother."

The joy of seeing Elijah suddenly turned into sorrow; the expression on her face was noticeable.

"Whatever happened to that cheerful smile?" Elijah asked.

"Patrick called."

"I'll call him as soon as I get something to eat," replied Elijah as he headed toward his room with his luggage.

"His brother, Prince, was killed while you were away."

Elijah's radiant look lost its illumination as he appeared saddened but composed. "What happened? Who did it?"

"I'm afraid no one knows, but he was found shot several times in the head. It was obvious the person who did it intended to kill him. I tried to reach you in Rome but with everything that has been going on I imagined you were busy. I think you should call Patrick as soon as you can. I believe the funeral is tomorrow."

"No, I'll go and see him right away. Would you put these things away for me, mother?"

"You go ahead; I'll take care of your things."

Half an hour later, Elijah was at his best friend's house. Patrick's sister Karen opened the door and greeted him with a hug as she burst into tears. Before long he was also greeted by Patrick, who together with his mother and father, Mr. and

Mrs. Reid, consoled Karen. Elijah expressed his regrets to the family and shortly was left alone with Patrick.

Elijah and Patrick walked outside by the pool in silence. Then Patrick spoke, his voice cracked from the sadness that burned like a torch in the midst of his heart. "He wouldn't listen. I told him—I *tried* to tell him that there is no life in drugs but he just wouldn't listen. 'Be quiet Cheetah,' he would say while he gave me one of his famous head locks and head rub. He called me Cheetah because for the longest time I used to think Cheetah was the name of the boy in old Tarzan films. That's what he told me; it wasn't until I got older that I found out that Cheetah was the chimpanzee. Since then I was always his little Cheetah; never once did he forget my birthday. Every year I got a gift, 'To my little brother Cheetah, from Tarzan.' Now he's gone just like that."

"I did not know him too well, but I am sure he will be missed."

"You once told me that there was no hell and that people who would normally go to hell would probably just cease to exist. How about my brother? Where do you think he'll go? I only ask you this now because of what the media have been reporting about you, claiming you to be the son of Christ. I must tell you, a lot of people think you are off your rocker."

"If the son of God in all his majestic glory was only accepted by a few, who am I to be accepted by all?"

"My brother lived a violent life; do you think he'll make it to Heaven? Or will he be one of those people who vaporize in the wind?" asked Patrick cynically.

"Oblivion is only for those whose deeds are beyond redemption."

"You mean like my brother?"

"I don't know, but a man who fails to enter my father's kingdom does not automatically lose his existence. If my father so chooses, he will give that person a second chance."

"What do you mean a second chance?"

"His soul will be cleansed by the eternal light, and on the day of that metamorphosis, he will once again be placed in a woman's womb."

"That sounds like reincarnation!" exclaimed Patrick.

"You see, Patrick, life after death is not as complex and mysterious as some people would have you believe. We are all from a holy circle, a light that illuminates an unimaginable brightness. In the midst of that light is our creator. Every time someone dies, depending on the outcome of his judgement, he will either go back to the holy circle, vaporize as you call it, or be reincarnated—using your own words, once again. Being a part of the holy circle is Heaven, and judgement day, like death, begins at birth. It is important that you understand, my friend, that God's ultimate goal for us is to have us be a part of that circle once again, because the more people become a part of it, the more complete he becomes."

"I thought God was perfect."

"Perfect but not complete."

"Wait a minute, man, you just lost me. You make it sound like God needs us more than we need him."

Elijah stared at Patrick for a while, almost as if he was somewhat reluctant to respond, but finally said, "You'll never know just how much."

Patrick and Elijah spent some more time talking about life and death. After a while, Patrick realized that the sense of loss he had felt was beginning to subside. He did not understand some of the things Elijah had said, but felt reassured by them.

*　　*　　*

The following morning, as the Reids gathered themselves to pay their final respect to their son Prince, they tried to seek comfort in the fact that the resolution of this nightmare was at hand. Many gathered in the Berean Church to say their good-byes. One by one they viewed Prince's body, shaking their heads in sadness. Many could not believe the horrifying way in which he died.

Patrick, Karen, and their parents stood over the body for ten minutes, crying as they kissed him good-bye before taking their seats. Soon thereafter, Angela, Prince's girlfriend, walked slowly toward the body with their three-year-old son in her arms. She glared at her child's father and within a few seconds rushed from the side of the casket and began vomiting. Guests who were seated in the front row hurried to her aid. They took the baby from her arms and assisted her as she stooped over, unable to control a part of her inside from coming out.

The line formed to view the body in the open casket, and as the line slowly moved, Mrs. McCloud, a lady who appeared to be in her late fifties, a very close friend of the family, stepped closer to pay her last respect. "Oh, my God," she said as she covered her mouth with her hands and fainted in the arms of her husband, who was standing in line behind her. Some of the spectators assisted him in placing her on the church bench so she could get some rest.

Mr. McCloud left his wife for a couple of minutes to see the body of a child whom he had watched grow up. Like a magnet, his eyes were glued to the body. He had an indescribable look on his face as he stared at the body, which was completely nude except for the tiny cloth which was covering the deceased's penis. The holes of the bullets and the damage done could be seen clearly because those areas were untouched by the mortician. Mr. McCloud saw the bloodstains that had thickened like clay on the body of a young man he had once told, "Someday you are going to be prime minister." His eyes were filled with tears as he wondered why the body of Prince had not been cleaned up and properly clothed.

McCloud's thoughts were interrupted by the Reverend, who gently moved him aside and closed the casket. "Ladies and gentlemen, please be seated for a while, then we'll continue with the viewing, allowing you to pay your last respect. But please be seated. I have something I think I should have announced earlier."

When they were all seated the Reverend continued. "It was the wish of the parents of the deceased that his body be left in the exact manner in which it was found. The private parts of the deceased have been covered up, but other than that, he is completely nude. The purpose for this blatant, unorthodox display can be found in three rationales. First, this viewing represents a symbolic gesture of the fact that we will return to our heavenly Father in the same manner in which he allows us to enter this world, with no worldly possession, not even the clothes we now wear on our backs. It is a reminder that the energy that we spend collecting and hoarding possessions in the world is futile, and that death will one day help us to pay testimony to this realization.

"Second, it serves to remind the young people, many of whom I have often tried to get to come to church but with little success, that drugs and the lifestyle that goes with them have serious and final consequences. It should serve as an awakening to both the young and the old that we have a serious problem and although it has not been characterized as it is in the United States, it is real.

"The third and final rationale for this type of viewing is to give you a chance to make a promise to yourself, a promise that upon witnessing the degree of the trauma that this man suffered, such catastrophe will not happen to you or your children. Burn his broken body into your hearts and never forget what lies ahead for those of you who are directly or indirectly responsible for the epidemic that now plagues our cities. I encourage all of you to come and pay your last respects to this man, regardless of what you may think of our method. His parents have sacrificed a small portion of his dignity so you can see the reality of the times. Honor them by listening and adhering to the message."

After most had viewed the body, Elijah walked towards the body while the whispers from among the people echoed to his every step. He stood there, his eyes pierced on Prince's body. He closed his eyes for a moment and uttered something in Latin beneath his breath, then he slowly opened his eyes again. It was as if for that moment someone had sent him a telegram telepathically. He walked over and sat beside Patrick.

"I am worried about Mom. She hasn't been able to cry since this ordeal started. Even when she viewed the body in the alley, she didn't shed a tear. As a matter of fact, she has been laughing and acting cheerful during this nightmare. I have never seen her behave this way before. I asked her how she was feeling and she said everybody should learn to accept death; it's part of life," Patrick whispered to Elijah.

"I see the wisdom in her statement, but like you question the feeling behind it," Elijah replied.

The sound of a temper tantrum coming from the line of guests waiting to view the body captured everyone's attention. They looked on as the three-year-old son of the deceased kept trying to break away from his mother. Finally she let him go to see where he would wander. He ran, pushing his way to the coffin, looking down on his father as he used one hand to gently slap his father's face, as if to say, "Wake up." He became calm again as his mother led him away. Five minutes later, he started acting up again, making body movements as if he wanted to see his father. His mother let him go once again and again he went to his father's coffin. "Da, da," he said as he continually hit the face of his deceased father. Realizing that his father was not responding, he went back to his mother's arms. Over and over he kept going back to the coffin in hopes that his father would acknowledge his presence, but finally he gave up and sat quietly by his mother's side.

Ten minutes before the closing of the coffin, the pastor once again encouraged all who wished to pay their last respects to Prince to come forward, because the casket would be closed soon. Patrick looked around the church and saw many people, most of them young men between the ages of seventeen and twenty-five. He knew by the way they dressed and looked they were also in the lifestyle of selling and using drugs.

"Thugs, all of them. I wouldn't be surprised if the person who killed him is right here looking at his handiwork. Creeps! Probably killed him over an ounce of dope," Patrick said angrily.

"Every era has its own parasite of the human spirit, but this is the worst I have ever seen it," Elijah replied.

Patrick looked at his sister, who was weeping. She turned around, looked over her shoulder, and said, "Patrick, they killed him. He was so good. Why did they have to kill him?"

Patrick did not know the answer to her question but felt compelled to sit beside her and console her as she shouted at the top of her voice, "Why did they have to kill him?"

The pastor was about to close the coffin, but before he could fully close it, a young man who appeared to be in his early teens walked up to view the body. The pastor allowed him to look briefly at the body, which he did for a couple of seconds before walking toward the entrance of the church.

Elijah got up immediately and walked toward the entrance as well. He saw the young man standing outside looking in all directions as if he were lost. "Do you believe in God?" Elijah asked the young man.

"Are you talking to me, mate?"

"Does it make you feel good to see your work one last time?"

"You're crazy, mate. I don't know what you are talking about."

"You killed him. But what makes it so bad is that you were supposed to be his friend,"

"You're crazy, mate. I didn't kill anybody."

"Do you believe in God?"

"Church is for sissies."

"Prepare to meet thy God, for you will meet him whether you are prepared or not," said Elijah as he walked away. Suddenly he stopped and stared at the young man. "By the way, before this month is over, you will die. The irony of it is that you will die the same way, by the hand of someone whom you have called friend and for the same reason: drugs."

*   *   *

After the burial, guests gathered at the Reids' residence for refreshments. Mrs. Reid was serving drinks and food as if it were a regular house party. She was laughing, making jokes, and being a perfect hostess.

"I am glad your mother is taking it so well," said Mr. Breeskin to Karen.

"Yes, she's a strong woman."

Moments later, the deceased's three-year-old son kicked one of the guests and was disciplined by his mother. "You're never to do that again," said Angela as she slapped him on the bottom.

The little boy ran toward his grandmother, "I am going to tell Dada," he said in his own embryonic, neologistic way. His unclear words sent a powerful chill through Mrs. Reid's body as she hugged him, broke out crying, and rushed upstairs.

Patrick and Karen ran after her. They watched her as she sat on the bed and wept harder and harder for her beloved son. It seemed like there was no end to her tears. Mrs. Reid started to hyperventilate. Her heart was pounding and her blood pressure shot up. Mr. Reid, who by now was by her side, called for an ambulance.

The paramedic who examined Mrs. Reid said her blood pressure had risen to 170 over 90. She told them that she had not taken her Lasix for her high blood pressure or her Thyroxine for her hyperthyroid. Instead she had been drinking brandy and various alcoholic beverages since the death of her son. The paramedics stabilized her and soon thereafter she was resting quietly.

An hour and a half later, many of the guests were getting ready to leave the Reids' residence, but were disgusted at what they discovered. Apparently someone had gone through all their coats and pocketbooks and emptied their purses and wallets, taking all the money and major credit cards.

"Who would do such a raunchy thing?" asked Karen.

"I told Mom not to let some of these thugs here," replied Patrick.

"My God, on a day like today you would think they would have the decency to be on their best behavior," interjected Mr. Reid. Mr. Reid apologized to his guests as they left one by one, frustrated and angry about the incident.

"I think I know who did it. It's Regina; she's a crackhead," said Ruby to Karen.

"Are you sure?"

"Yeah, I'm sure. She's the only one who would do something like this."

"Where is she?"

"She left early, but don't worry, my buddies and I will find her," Ruby replied. Ruby left the Reids' residence.

Less than an hour later Ruby returned with a paper bag in her hand. In the paper bag were all the guests' credit cards and most of the cash that had been stolen.

"How did you get—?" Before Karen could complete the question, Ruby told her the entire story of how she and her friends confronted Regina at the Emery Park and were able to recover the stolen items. Karen gave her a hug and thanked her, only to notice that Ruby had a slight grin on her face while leaving.

"What's so funny?"

"It's Regina."

"What about her?"

"She had seven dollars stuck up her vagina." Karen and Ruby both laughed aloud and for a second or two that humor brought back a forgotten joy.

Elijah, knowing that he would never see Patrick again, bid him farewell as both friends walked outside. "Are you alright?" Elijah asked.

"I am going to miss Prince. We spent so many times joking that I never really got a chance to let him know how much I loved him and admired him, even though he wasn't always doing the right thing."

"I am   э he knows."

"Thanks for coming, Elijah, and for always being a good friend."

Elijah took a chain with a crucifix on it and handed it to Patrick. "Remember me always."

"It's beautiful, thanks. But what do you mean I should remember you? Are you leaving again?"

"Yes, and I am not coming back."

"What do you mean you are not coming back? Are you moving away from London?"

"I guess you could say that."

Patrick sensed that Elijah would rather not talk about it further. The two friends hugged. As Elijah began to walk away, he said, "One more thing, Patrick. Have you told your parents about your medical problem?"

"No, not yet. With all this happening I don't know if I can. I am taking my medication and hoping for the best. That's all I can do, right?"

Elijah walked back closer to Patrick and placed his right hand on Patrick's head.

"You are not going to baptize me, are you?"

Elijah did not respond. Instead, he closed his eyes and said, "Father! glorify me that I may glorify you. Restore his health so that in the midst of this ordeal comes a victory."

The clouds began to move rapidly across the sky as thunder and lightning became more and more obvious by their sounds. Elijah prayed on as Patrick became a little anxious about the drastic change in the weather.

"You're cured through the loving grace of God."

Before Patrick could say anything, a bright light came over Elijah's body and blinded his sight for a second. Patrick held his eyes and within seconds opened them to see that Elijah was gone. He knew it was humanly impossible for anyone to leave without being seen because of the openness of the view, but had to face the reality of his experience. Patrick ran inside his house, and although he never drank before, poured himself several glasses of red wine. Then he opened his palm and noticed the crucifix Elijah had given him. He saw the crucifix branded in the middle of his palm, almost as if someone had taken a hot iron and branded him. He was speechless as he poured himself another glass of wine.

*   *   *

A few days later, Patrick tried to call Elijah but was told

157

by the operator that the telephone number he called had been disconnected for years. "Operator, there must be some mistake. I have been calling that number for the longest time. I have even *made* calls from that number."

"I am sorry, sir, but according to our records no telephone line has been connected to that address for the last fifteen years."

"Are you looking up 425 Edmond Avenue?" Patrick asked in exasperation.

"Yes sir!"

"Thank you," Patrick said as he replaced the receiver.

The next day, Patrick waited patiently in his doctor's office. He was awaiting the results of another blood test. Although he had been having doubts about whether Elijah was merely a figment of his imagination, Patrick felt it would do no harm to have another test, just in case. Patrick's thoughts were interrupted by his physician, Dr. Sinclair.

"Patrick, are you okay?"

"Hi, doctor."

"I ran the tests as you requested, both the ELISA and the Western blot, and I don't understand it. According to these results, you don't have the HIV virus. I don't understand how we could have made such an error. I was so certain. I am sorry, Patrick. I know what it must have been like for you."

Patrick slowly walked out of the hospital in daze while Dr. Sinclair tried to explain what might have happened. He looked at the branded crucifix in the palm of his hands and smiled. "Thank you, Elijah, son of the Messiah. I will remember you always."

19

Elijah's popularity preceded him to the United States. News of his arrival spread like wildfire throughout the nation. Everyone waited with anticipation and curiosity to see this young man who claimed to be the son of the Messiah.

While Elijah was preparing to speak on the Monument grounds, back in Rome Father Andropolus called another special meeting with his colleagues. They met in the same room where they had conspired to kill the pope. This time they had a fifth partner to their conspiracy. The failed attempt to kill the pope had brought forth an even more urgent crisis in their eyes. There was a quietness that gave birth to the nesting of a holy evil as Father Andropolus spoke.

"First of all, let me take the time to thank you, Mr. President, for coming from the United States to be a part of this essential meeting."

"There is no need to thank me, Father Andropolus; this young man is becoming a concern to many of us political leaders. He has millions of people following him, but what concerns me most, and this is not to say that I am prejudiced, is that he's Black. If he were to run for the presidency someday, only God knows what spell he might cast on the American people."

"Well, that's why we are here: to decide what needs to be done about him," replied Father Andropolus.

"What happens if he is truly a child sent by God?" asked Father Francis.

"He is the devil, that's who he is," replied Father Andropolus.

"But surely the miracles and the wonders that he has performed could only have come from God," interjected Father Andrew.

"Even Lucifer possesses powers that far exceeded man's imagination," said Father Andropolus.

"I really don't give a damn who he is. The only thing I am concerned about is what we are going to do to neutralize his popularity," said the president.

"Not just his popularity; this boy is a danger to society and to every religious doctrine. We must put a stop to him once and for all," said Father Andropolus.

They struggled within themselves to reach a consensus as to who should carry out the assassination. Father Andropolus thought the president should see that it was done, and the president thought that Father Andropolus and his colleagues should do it. They sat there for over two hours debating why each thought it would be best that the other carried out the assassination. Father Andropolus got up and went outside. Minutes later he came back with a bag.

"Mr. President, in this bag are two marbles, a red and a blue. Choose a color and if you pick your color from the bag, then I will make the necessary arrangements," said Father Andropolus.

"I feel like a schoolboy," said the president. He put his hand in the bag with the hope that he would get blue, but he picked the red marble instead.

"I guess this means I get to do the dirty work," said the president.

"If it's any consolation, you'll be doing God's work in addition to saving us a trip," said Father Andropolus with a smile.

"Not that I don't trust you, but would you mind very much letting me see the other marble?" asked the President. Without saying a word, Father Andropolus showed him a blue marble. They all laughed aloud.

A day later the president was back in the United States. He had contacted the director of the CIA, John Peterson, for a private meeting. They sat in the Oval Office chatting about each other's families, drinking coffee, and talking about the stresses that come with each other's jobs.

Then out of the blue the president made a pitch. "Peterson,

I want you to kill somebody for me, or at least arrange to have it done; either way, I don't care. I just want it done."

Peterson paused for a moment, then said as he laughed, "You almost got me, Mr. President. Kill someone for you! No one can accuse you of not having a sense of humor, Mr. President."

The president was serious. Peterson, realizing this, said, "You're joking, of course. Right, Mr. President?"

"I never joke about killing a person, especially on an empty stomach."

"You're serious. You really want to kill someone?"

"No, I want you to kill someone for me."

"But who? And what on Earth for?"

"Have you heard of Elijah?"

"That's the kid some people are calling a prophet, another Christ. Wait a minute; you can't be serious. You really don't think this kid is a threat to society, do you, Mr. President?"

"It doesn't matter what I think; what matters is what the American people believe, especially the Blacks who are convinced that he is their savior. You're not hitting the sauce anymore, are you, Peterson?"

Peterson was surprised and somewhat disappointed that the president would ask such a question, when he knew full well that he had not had a drink in over three years. "No, Mr. President. As they teach us in AA, take it one day at a time, sometimes even one step at a time."

"Good, that's good. I remember how the big boys tried to sabotage your confirmation when I tried to get you this job. I'm sure glad things are working out."

Peterson hung his head because once again he was experiencing an old behavior of the president. Every time the president wanted a personal favor off the record, he would remind Peterson of how he got the job.

"This young man is a threat to everything we hold dear, Peterson. We simply cannot let him go on disturbing the social order of things."

161

"My wife and I have listened to him. He's just a kid. He's not even in politics."

"Yes, but what happens when that kid becomes a man? He's already creating an uproar amongst Blacks. The last thing we need is another Black Power era like in the sixties."

Peterson left the Oval Office agreeing to carry out the president's wishes. He was not to share this dark secret with anyone, not even his wife, otherwise he too would pay the ultimate price. Distraught by the situation, Peterson's hands shook uncontrollably as he tried to open his car door. After fidgeting with it for a few minutes, he finally steadied his hand enough to insert the key in the lock. Trying to start the car was also a task. Frustrated, he banged his head several times on the steering wheel, and only stopped when he noticed that blood had started to flow from his forehead.

Get a grip, old boy, Peterson thought to himself. *Why am I so nervous about offing this kid? It's not as if I have never done this before. Shucks, I don't even have to do it myself; I can always get one of my flunkies.* His thoughts calmed him just enough for him to get the keys in the ignition.

Peterson drove around for a while, then stopped in front of Misty's, a local hangout for when one wanted to be incognito. With his car engine running, he sat in front of the bar for five minutes and just stared at the entrance. Shortly thereafter, he got out and went inside. People inside the bar focused their attention on Peterson as they noticed blood dripping off his forehead, something that he was apparently not aware of anymore. Peterson sat on a nearby stool on the far right corner of the bar.

"Are you alright, mister?" asked the bartender.

"Double Courvoisier on the rocks and keep it coming until I tell you to stop."

"Sure, mister. The bathroom is back there if you want to clean up a bit."

Peterson touched his forehead and saw the blood on his fingers. "Yeah, right. Thanks. Thanks a lot." He walked in the direction of the bathroom. On his return from the bathroom, Peterson headed toward the door.

"Hey, mister, what about your drink?" yelled the bartender above the music and laughter.

Peterson turned, and then remembered that he had come inside to have a drink. He walked back toward the bar and found the stool he had previously occupied. He took out his wallet, handed the bartender a twenty. As he waited for his change, his eyes caught a picture of the president on the wall behind the bartender. Like someone suffering from brief reactive psychosis, he swiftly picked up the glass of Courvoisier from the counter and tossed it at the president's picture. "Son of a bitch," he said as the picture went crashing to the floor.

"I don't know what the hell the problem is, but leave right now or I'll call the cops," said the bartender.

Peterson rested his face in the palm of his hands, then turned toward the exit. "Keep the change. Sorry," he said as he departed.

*　　*　　*

It had been a week since the conspiracy to kill Elijah was orchestrated. Still, Elijah was travelling around the nation's capital making guest appearances on TV talk shows, doing anything that would help the people to understand the reason for accepting him as a part of their lives. Seeking solitude and rest at an empty AME church, he sat down in his usual lotus position, facing the cross before him. In a higher plane of cosmic consciousness, he began talking in Hebrew to entities that could not be seen by the human eye, but who nevertheless bathed him with their holy presence.

An hour later, Elijah heard a voice. "I was there at your birth."

Elijah did not seem startled. His head was still hung, his eyes closed, and a few seconds went by before he responded. "Which one?"

"Your father would sit like that for hours. Ironically, I believe the first time I met him he was in the same position that you are in right now," commented the voice.

Elijah got up and faced the person to whom the voice belonged.

"You have grown into a fine young man. Your father would be pleased with what you have accomplished. Forgive a foolish old man. I am Father Andreas, a dear friend of your mother and father."

"How did you find me?" asked Elijah.

"Your presence is felt all over; it was not hard. But enough of that, tell me how have you been?" said Father Andreas as he took Elijah by the shoulder and walked him over where they both could sit down.

"I am pleased with the work I am doing for my father."

They talked for a while, then Father Andreas made Elijah promise that he would meet him the next day at St. Margaret Church at 8:30 P.M. He told Elijah that it was a matter of life and death, but he could not go into detail until the time they would meet again at the church. Elijah agreed that he would be there.

*   *   *

Elijah got to the church as planned. The gigantic church was empty. He sat down and kept looking around, then he saw a Bible on the seat beside him. He opened it casually, as the wind blew the pages. Then as the wind stopped, the pages of the Bible stood still as if they were glued to that one passage.

Elijah read the passage to himself, Mark chapter 14, verses 43 through 46: "And immediately, while he yet spake, cometh Judas, one of the twelve, and with him a great multitude with swords and staves, from the chief priests and the scribes and the elders. And he that betrayed him had given them a token, saying, whomever I shall kiss, that same is he. Take him and lead him away safely. And as soon as he was come, he goeth straight way to him, and saith, Master, Master and kissed him. And they laid their hands on him and took him."

When Elijah was through reading the Scripture and became fully aware of the revelation, he kissed the Bible and said, "If it is your will again, O God." He heard footsteps and saw Father Andreas approaching. Elijah got up and met him halfway down the aisle.

Father Andreas looked at Elijah, then hung his head. "Forgive me, my son," he said, almost as if he was ashamed. Before he could fully ask for Elijah's forgiveness, Peterson emerged with a gun in his right hand and a bottle of Courvoisier in his left. Elijah looked at him and remained silent as the ordeal continued to develop.

"The president and Father Andropolus promised they would bring me to Rome if I helped them. Do you know what that means? All my life I have been dreaming of something like this," said Father Andreas.

"At least Judas had the grace not to defile my father's house," said Elijah as he looked around the church.

Peterson, with trembling hands, moved quickly and hit Elijah over the head with the gun. Elijah fell to the ground unconscious.

"Is he dead?" asked Father Andreas.

"Not yet," replied Peterson as he picked up Elijah and threw him over his shoulder.

"Where are you taking him?"

"You have done your part, now let me do mine, priest," said Peterson, and he took Elijah away.

Father Andreas sat down on a bench, leaned over, and picked up the Bible. The passage that Elijah was reading was undisturbed by the incident. Father Andreas became breathless as he read Judas's betrayal of Christ. "My God! He knew what I was about to do!"

20

"I don't want him dead. Find out who the devil he is and whether or not he is as dangerous as some people think. I'm leaving you two men, the only people who are cleared to enter this room. Do you understand?" asked Peterson.

"Sure, sure Peterson. But everyone knows this kid. He is suffering from delusions of grandeur but he's no threat to society."

"See if you can convince him that being another king would be bad for his health. Find out as much about him as possible. I'll be in touch. One more thing, only you and Bert should have keys to this door. No one goes in or out without your approval."

"Don't worry, Peterson. Have I ever let you down? Don't answer that," said Dr. Weinstein with a smile.

Peterson leaned against the nearby door for support as he watched his friend Weinstein take long strides down the hallway. Weinstein and Peterson had been close friends for many years. They had been there for each other through the highs and lows. Weinstein had served as Peterson's confidante on many undercover operations that gave Peterson the creeps. But this one was shrouded in just too much secrecy. Peterson had said too little in entrusting this young man to Weinstein's care. This only piqued Weinstein's curiosity even more. As Weinstein pondered the task that lay ahead, he pulled on his beard, which had just enough grey in it to give him that distinguished look against his otherwise boyish face, even though he had recently celebrated his forty-fifth birthday.

Meanwhile, Elijah lay unconscious in the sparsely furnished room. Peterson had thought it was a stroke of genius when he brought Elijah to St. Elizabeth's so that Weinstein could give him a workover. If anyone could figure what demon was in Elijah, Weinstein could.

Weinstein walked into the room with a tray of food in his hands. Elijah quickly sat up on one side of the bed. Elijah stared at Weinstein, who was dressed in a white coat, looking as if he worked in a lab. Weinstein's manner was that of a calm and quiet man. Without saying a word and with a pleasant smile, he handed Elijah the tray of food. He then pulled up a chair and watched Elijah as he ate. He looked Elijah over from head to toe, as if he was wondering what made this eighteen-year-old kid so dangerous.

"My name is Dr. Weinstein. I am a psychiatrist. I would like to ask you a few questions. Would that be okay with you?"

Minutes later, Elijah placed the tray on the floor beside him then sat with his hands on his knees.

"I see you were hungry. I could get you some more if you would like—after you answer a few questions for me, of course," said Dr. Weinstein. Elijah did not respond but sat there and looked at the doctor. An hour had come and gone and still Dr. Weinstein was unable to get Elijah to say a word.

"People are saying that you are the Antichrist, much more so than the Christ. I think they are probably right. What do you think?" Again, Elijah did not respond and Dr. Weinstein grew frustrated as he took off his glasses and wiped the sweat that was beginning to fog up his view. He thought his ears were deceiving him when Elijah overcame his selective mutism and spoke.

"When one's accusation is based on suspicions and not facts, then it is the privilege of the accused to always ignore the ignorance of the accusers."

"For a minute there I thought I was hallucinating," said Dr. Weinstein jokingly as he continued his psychoanalysis of Elijah. "Tell me, where are your parents? Who are you and why are you here? Where exactly did you come from?"

"If the prophesy of the yesterdays were enough to secure man's existence today, I would not be here. So why do you ask me about the past?"

"Because to untangle the mystery of the spider's web, one must always retrace the steps of the spider. It is as if you popped out of thin air. No one seems to know anything about you. People say you have worked miracles, yet here you are being held against your will. How do you feel about that?"

Elijah became silent once again as the doctor got up from his chair, paced around the floor for a while, then tried another approach with Elijah. "Let's talk about God since, after all, you are the Christ. Is it true that man has the choice between hell or heaven?"

"Free will is the essence of man's salvation."

"But is it not true that God forewarned us that failure to comply with his wishes can lead to hell, which in my opinion is a form of contingency control. If I tell my son not to leave the house because if he does he will not be allowed to drive the car for a month, indeed, he may not leave the house because he knows what will be the outcome of his action. This is a means of controlling his behavior. The fact that I placed a variable intact that would prevent him from exercising full autonomy over his action limits his ability to exercise free will. Couldn't you make the same analogy with God and man in terms of hell? We can choose to participate in any endeavor, but if we don't make the right choice then we may end up in that hot place."

"There is no hell, but there are consequences for our actions. In your scenario, your son still has the freedom to choose. Regardless of the decision he makes, there will be consequences to his actions. Still the choice will be his."

"But don't you think that people are being forced by God to do things against their will?"

"If such was the case, the world would have been a better place."

Dr. Weinstein felt he had distracted Elijah long enough to have gained his trust. "Elijah, we have a problem of a sensitive nature and would like you to help us. You do like to help people in need, don't you?"

"When I can."

"Not since Martin Luther King's days has there been so much solidarity among Blacks. They are calling you the 'Black Messiah' who's come back to convince the white race that Christ was indeed a Black man. This newfound Black pride has reenergized the Civil Rights movements to new heights. Hell, in this upcoming election they are even talking about putting a Black in the White House."

"What do you want of me?"

"Simple. Have a public gathering with your people and reassure them that you are not the Christ and in no way related to God. Let them see how ludicrous the entire thing sounds."

"To do this would be to reject the prophesy and deny my destiny. No, doctor, neither you nor the government can make me do this."

Dr. Weinstein smiled with his usual crooked grin and began pacing around the room again. He stopped a foot from Elijah, took off his glasses and began cleaning them once again. "I understand your convictions, Elijah, and I do respect you for them," he said, then with a swift movement of his hand across Elijah's face sent Elijah crashing to the floor on the other side of the room.

"Do you think this is a goddamn game, boy?" he said as he watched Elijah wipe the blood from his mouth and nose. "You see, Elijah, no matter what you do, there will always be evil in the world."

"Evil is the manifestation of man's imperfection, doctor," replied Elijah as he got up and sat back on the side of the bed.

"You better be willing to change your attitude tomorrow when I return. You see, Elijah, we like the way things are. We throw your people a bone now and then by appointing them to a position here and there. Everybody is happy with that. We will not allow some wet behind the ears kid suffering from delusions of grandeur to mess with the status quo. It's important that you understand, Elijah. I'll do whatever is necessary to change your mind. And believe me, I'm good at what I do; that's why you were brought here."

"Does that include killing?"

"Yes."

" 'I will use treatment to help the sick according to my ability and judgement, but never with a view to injury or wrongdoing. Neither will I administer a poison to anybody when asked to do so, nor will I suggest such a course. But I will keep pure and holy both my life and my art. Into whatsoever houses I enter, I will enter to help the sick, and I will abstain from all intentional wrongdoing and harm, especially from abusing the bodies of man or woman, bond or free. I will never divulge, holding such things to be holy secrets. Now if I carry out this oath, and break it not, may I gain forever reputation among all men for my life and for my art; but if I transgress it and forswear myself, may the opposite befall me,' " Elijah recited from the Hippocratic Oath.

The doctor nodded, impressed with Elijah's knowledge of the Oath. He ran his hand through his hair then immediately put both hands in his coat pockets, acting as if he was about to have a panic attack. "We all have our demons, Elijah."

"Demons are entities that oppose God, doctor. Somehow I don't see you as someone who is against God but rather someone who is a prisoner of others' emotions and approval. You are so concerned about what people think and feel about you that you are willing to kill to gain that acknowledgment."

"Well, don't concern yourself. It's enough that you understand. Just like you said, I'll do whatever is necessary for my country. I'll be back tomorrow. For your sake, I sincerely hope you'll have a change of attitude."

Thirty minutes later Elijah received a visit from two muscular Secret Service men, Bert and Norris, and a nurse. The nurse had a hypodermic needle in her hand. Realizing her intentions, Elijah rolled up his sleeve in readiness for the injection.

"That's a good boy," the nurse said as she withdrew the needle from Elijah's arm and wiped it with a piece of cotton. "I'll be back within four hours to give you another one of these. This is to help you get a good night's rest."

"So why wake me to give me another one since I would already been sleeping?"

The nurse looked at Bert and Norris, trying to find an answer to Elijah's question. "Never mind. The doctor wants you to have a shot every four hours until he sees you tomorrow," replied the nurse angrily.

Throughout the night the nurse kept coming to Elijah's room every four hours just as she said she would. She was alarmed, however, when on each of her trips to Elijah's room, he was sitting up on one side of the bed with his sleeves rolled up waiting for his routine injection. The clouded consciousness of a lonely entity embraced the light of the sun as it struggled to comfort him by attempting to penetrate the thickness of the window to his room. Filled with the pressure of the entire world, Elijah folded his arms and hung his head down. His body began to rock back and forth as if he was a drug addict going through withdrawal.

A few hours later, Dr. Weinstein, Bert, and Norris entered Elijah's room only to find him semi-unconscious across the bed.

"What's the matter with him?" asked Bert.

"His body apparently couldn't handle the potency of the drug. Damn it! I told you guys that using the drug while it is still in its experimental stage could be dangerous. Bureaucrats!" said the doctor angrily as he tried to revive Elijah.

"Look, he's coming around," Bert said.

"Elijah, Elijah, can you hear me?" asked the doctor as he slapped Elijah across the face gently.

"Monique, I love you," said Elijah in his delirious state.

"Monique? Who the hell is Monique?" asked Norris.

"I don't know. Must be his girlfriend, or grandmother. How the hell am I supposed to know?" asked the doctor, annoyed. "Elijah, can you hear me? Where are you now, Elijah?"

"Pennsylvania. Erie, Pennsylvania," replied Elijah almost incoherently.

"Erie, Pennsylvania! He's really out of it," said Bert.

"Concentrate, Elijah. What is today's date?" Dr. Weinstein asked.

"February 3, 1950."

"1950! Now I know his mind is gone," said Norris.

"Will you both shut up!" Dr. Weinstein shouted to the Secret Service men. "How am I suppose to conduct my examination with all this chatting?" Turning back to Elijah, the doctor continued. "Who are you? What is your name?"

"Finkenauer," replied Elijah as he passed out.

"It's no use; let him rest for a while," said Dr. Weinstein. The three men left the room, talking about the impact the drug had on Elijah. Suddenly it was as if lightning struck Dr. Weinstein. His heart started to palpitate as if it were trying to jump out of his chest. The clipboard fell from his hand as he ran back quickly to Elijah's room. Without knowing what was wrong, Bert and Norris followed behind him. Dr. Weinstein tried to open the door, but the keys fell to the ground. "Damn it," he said before finally opening up the door. They went inside, only to find an empty room.

"Where is he, doctor?" Bert asked.

"I don't know," replied the doctor as he sat on the side of the bed.

"Somebody must have let him out. Hell, he couldn't have just vanished into thin air," said Norris at the top of his voice.

"How many other people have keys to this room?" shouted Bert.

"Just you and I. The nurse uses my key," Weinstein replied.

"Holy shit! You mean he just got up and disappeared?" asked Agent Norris.

"More than that, Agent Norris. February 3, 1950 was the day I was born. Erie, Pennsylvania, is my birthplace. I have been away from home so long that it didn't even dawn on me until I left the room," said Dr. Weinstein.

"Who is Finkenauer?" asked Bert.

"That's my mother's maiden name."

"Holy shit! Who the hell is this kid?" asked Bert.

"I don't know, but if he is who he says he is, I don't think we should miss church on Sunday," said Dr. Weinstein.

21

It was now 4:00 P.M. and thousands of people of all races had gathered on the grounds of the Washington Monument to hear the young man who proclaimed himself to be the son of the Messiah. Many thought he would not show up, while others *hoped* he would not. Anticipation and speculation filled the souls of the crowd who waited to see and hear Elijah. Some believed he was truly the son of the Messiah while others' hearts were filled with doubt; still they gathered to hear him out of curiosity. Fulfilling his promise, they found Elijah in the midst of them.

The crowd grew impatient as a gentleman who was sitting on a blanket said, "I've come a long way to hear you preach. So when are you going to get the show on the road?"

"I did not come here to preach."

"Then what the hell have you gotten us here for?"

"I did not come here to preach or persuade, for the prophets before me and clergy of today have done well in this regard."

"Then why the bloody hell are you here then, mate?"

Elijah walked up close to the man, stooped down, his nose only inches from the man's face, and said, "To enlighten. Had you had power you would have known this."

"And what is this power you speak of?"

"The ability to embrace humility as a friend and patience as a brother."

The gentleman turned away from Elijah and picked up a book that was lying next to him. Elijah looked around and shook his head at the number of people that were still streaming onto the Monument grounds.

"Young man, can you hear me?" asked an elderly lady as she tried to use her hands to clear the path.

"As I stood in the midst of fire and felt myself as cold as ice; as I seldom listen to thunder but rather to the rain on a stormy night, so is it with your voice and the gathering of my people," responded Elijah. They smiled at each other.

"It's been a long time since anyone has made me smile," said the elderly lady.

"What is your name?" asked Elijah.

"Mrs. Brown."

"Why do you choose to deprive the world of such a wonderful smile, Mrs. Brown?"

"I am eighty-two years old, and I am scared."

"Of what are you afraid?"

"Of dying; I do not want to die."

"You are angry at God for your having been born, and you are sad that there will come a time when you will die."

She slapped her cheek with her right hand. "Yes, that's it right there. I couldn't have said it any better." She continued to talk about how she could not understand why is it that she had to die after working so hard to achieve the things she had. "It's so unfair!" she said.

"There is an old saying, 'Everybody wants to go to Heaven, but nobody wants to die.' This place was not intended to be the final resting place for humanity. And no man can get to the other side of the ocean without first leaving where he stands."

"I understand. But why do I feel this way?"

"Greed!"

The crowd went in an uproar because they thought Elijah was being rude. He raised his right hand above his head, slowly unclenching his fist as his command for silence was granted. "Greed is like an insatiable thirst. Whatever we seek, we seek abundantly, with little concern for those who have less. So is it with life. Yes, I can see how you may think it is unfair, but why would you pack all your belongings on a ship being fully aware that your destination is temporary, then become angry at the knowledge that you will need to unload your belongings while remaining at your temporary place of rest. Rejoice that our Heavenly Father has created you from nothing and has made it possible for you to feel, taste, smell, see, and hear the essence of life and has promised you this throughout eternity. What else can anyone ask for that would not be considered a sign of greed?" Elijah kissed Mrs. Brown on the forehead.

Then he continued. "Many of you have asked yourselves, could this truly be the second coming? My question to you is, what is the second coming? If you think the second coming is to take away the good and allow the bad to dwell in eternal life, then this is not the second coming. If you think the second coming is to bring a new inner peace to man with the intention of acknowledging that we are all God's children, then this is the second coming. If you think the second coming is to behold the Heavenly Father coming from the sky, then this is not the second coming. If you think the second coming is to behold the wonders performed by the son of the Messiah, then this is the second coming. If you think the second coming is to cast sinners into brimstone and fire, then this is not the second coming. If you think the second coming is to strengthen the bond between man and God, then this is the second coming. If you think the second coming is to raise the dead and allow them to walk the earth once again, then this is not the second coming. If you think the second coming is to forgive the transgressions of men so that they may gain favor in the eyes of God, which will allow them to enter the gates of Heaven, then this is the second coming. The second coming is different things to all men but with one constraint; it is the day and hour when I, the son of the Messiah, was sent by God to bear testimony to what is. Many of you have asked if I am truly the son of the Messiah or a representative sent by Lucifer. I say this to you my brothers and sisters, that you will know the answer to your questions by my deeds. For as you have found no fault within my Father, neither will you find any in me."

Before Elijah could continue, someone from the crowd shouted, "Are you saying you are perfect?" The question brought laughter from some of the people.

Elijah was quiet for a while and then he answered the question. "How can I show you the path to an entity which is the epitome of perfection if I too am not a part of that realm, as you too can be? Many of you have asked if I am here to save the world from destruction and my answer to this question is no. Rather, I am here to save you from yourselves. I know all your questions and the answers to them all. The son of the Messiah is not here to make the world a better place for you; rather to make you a better person for the world. For the world was evil from the beginning of time and it must remain so even until the end."

Elijah was again interrupted by a scream coming from the crowd. "Liar, liar," said a voice. He stopped and looked in the direction where the voice came from and then he slowly walked amongst the crowd until he came to a woman who seemed distressed that though her child had seen Elijah, he was still in pain and was unable to walk due to his malformed figure.

"You said you would heal my son," said the old woman to Elijah. "But you lied. Look at him; he is still in pain. Why did you lie? We came all the way from Amsterdam because we thought you were a child sent from God, but you are nothing but a liar. You are the devil," she said to Elijah angrily.

"You came expecting a miracle, but you did not bring your faith with you," said Elijah.

Still indignant, the woman looked at Elijah as if she wished he were a cockroach so she could crush him with her heel. Then she spoke: "So my faith doesn't measure up to Christ's. What are you going to do, sue me?"

"You speak of the measurement of faith, something of which you apparently know little." Elijah felt the woman's rage, and though it overwhelmed his spirit, he was more concerned about her misconception of Christ's faith. He looked over his shoulders and saw a ten-year-old boy with his father.

"Do you see that young boy with his father?" Elijah asked the woman. She looked over her shoulders and saw the young boy, who clung to his father's leg, knowing that strangers' eyes were on him.

"My father's faith shivers in the presence of that boy's, for Christ's faith comes from the power of knowing, allowing him to see the light at the end of the tunnel. But the boy's faith comes from only believing in the words of God. The content of his faith is the beam that will become the light at the end of the tunnel. No, my dear lady, I do not ask you to possess the Messiah's faith, but to use it as a stepping stone to strengthen your own."

The woman looked at her son and stroked his hair as tears came rushing down her face, leaving many to wonder why Elijah seemed so indifferent to her weeping.

"Have you no heart? Can't you see the poor woman is in pain?" yelled a male spectator.

Elijah turned to him and whispered, "Do not confuse her pain with her tears, for a woman's tears serve three purposes: to convince, to distract, and to evoke sympathy. Finding the source of each is a revelation within itself. So in defending a woman's honor, make sure the honor in question is worthy of defending."

Like a subway train, after a passenger has pulled the emergency lever, the woman's tears came to an immediate stop upon hearing Elijah's words.

The woman's son was still visibly in pain. His sad eyes looked up at Elijah. Elijah looked at him, held his hands, then he looked at the woman who had accused him of lying and deceiving her and many others and he said, "Woman, look around you and tell me what do you see."

The woman looked around and saw to her amazement many people shouting at the top of their voices that they had been healed. They were giving praise to God in their own way. It was a happy and joyous crowd. Then she looked at her son and then at Elijah and said, "I don't understand; why wasn't my son healed?"

"You came to see the son of the Messiah but you did not bring your faith with you." Elijah turned and looked at the boy once again, still holding on to his hand, then he uttered in a soft and gentle voice, "The time has come when the daughters

177

will no longer bear the sins of their mothers and where sons will no longer bear the sins of their fathers, for this is within the prophesy." He squeezed the young man's hand tightly as he used the other and gently caressed the boy from his head to his toe.

Suddenly the boy's body jerked, and to the child's amazement and that of others around, his malformed body became straight and the pain left him. The boy smiled with relief. His eyes reflected a new strength. Elijah slowly raised him to his feet; he had a big smile on his face as he hugged Elijah. The people in the immediate area knelt down and worshipped Elijah. Elijah looked at the woman once again and without another word started to walk away. She felt embarrassed as she asked, "Why did you help my son even after I accused you of being the devil?"

"Woman, there is no boundary to God's love. For so it is with me as it was with my father when the Romans tried, persecuted him, and watched in silence, not understanding his ways. Your son has been restored to health. Give your thanks to the heavenly Father, for I am only His instrument."

Elijah turned to the crowd again and said, "What I am about to say to you will make you wonder whether or not I am indeed a man of God. But I have seen the wickedness of men and in their deeds they have rationalized it as if Lucifer was the precipitating factor; they engaged in unholy acts. I say this to you: many times Lucifer is asleep when you commit these insidious acts. For whatever you do, you will not escape the wrath of the heavenly Father by telling him that Lucifer is responsible for your sins. I tell you these things that you will know that you will be held accountable for every single thing you do on this earth. Although you were told that there was no price for salvation, the son of the Messiah just said there is."

Before Elijah could continue, a voice from the crowd screamed, "And what is this price we must pay for salvation?"

Elijah looked up at the sky for a while and for a second or two was quiet, then he said, "The purity of your own heart."

"And how will we know when our hearts are pure?"

178

"Just as you feel the wind on your skin, so will it be when the blood of my father cleanses your heart and makes you whole. For the purity of which I speak will not only be accomplished by deeds but by total acceptance of my father and me."

Elijah closed his eyes, raised his hands to the heavens, and began to pray. "Heavenly Father, whose mercy and kindness far extend and exceed what we deserve. Grant us the courage that we may come to know the truth and receive it. Help them, O God, to understand the nature of your peace, that in doing so they will show more love and kindness and less hatred and hostility toward one another. Bless them, O God, for their ways are far from being perfect. Help them to remember and realize that they were made in our image, the image of perfection. Instill in them, O God, the ability to seek, to explore beyond the heavens, but not without acknowledging that their findings and wisdom are gifts from you and that the utilization of this type of knowledge can better serve only you, our heavenly Father. Forsake them not for their sins, even though these are many."

As he continued to pray, a strange dark cloud moved across the sky and the thunder roared, almost as if the heavenly staff were acknowledging his prayer. Then the once silent crowd became noisy as fingers were pointed at Elijah's head. There were questions amongst them, questions of great concern, for as people continued to point at Elijah's head, they noticed the halo. They confirmed within their hearts that he must truly be the son of the Messiah. And as he continued to pray even harder, a light surrounded his entire body as people looked at him and were mystified, to say the least, as they tried to resolve the enigma of this unusual entity who stood before them on behalf of his Father and the heavenly staff in hopes that by fulfilling the prophesy he would once again extend their time, a time of redemption.

Elijah stayed at the Monument for hours as he tried to teach the people and give them insight not only into their lives but also in the life of God. They listened attentively, but sometimes their minds wandered off to the miracles that their sons, daughters, uncles, and other family members experienced under the guidance of this youth who stood before them. Not before long, as they slowly departed from the Monument, they were shouting and praising, and people once lame and blind or who from birth had afflictions cast on them, were now singing and dancing. This was a day of miracles, a day when the son of the Messiah lifted up his hands and asked the heavenly Father to forgive and to forget. Elijah watched them as they wandered and scattered all over the place in great praise to the heavenly Father, and uttered to himself, "Father, thank you for showing them the true meaning of love."

And as days went by, Elijah came to be one of the most popular and well-known figure in the world. His deeds and his teachings, his miracles and the places he visited caught the attention of millions. People from all over the world travelled thousands of miles just to get a glimpse of this young man who proclaimed himself the son of the Messiah. He carried out significant and meaningful deeds that removed all doubt that he was indeed the son of the Messiah.

22

After hours of speaking to a multitude of people, which had become Elijah's daily agenda, he grew tired. Many watched as he rested his eyes. Some used the time to meet their physical needs. But Elijah's rest was soon interrupted when he felt a hand on his shoulder. Elijah opened his eyes and was confronted by a priest who introduced himself as Father Owens. He looked in Elijah's eyes for a while, almost as if he were searching for something far beyond what he was seeing.

Father Owens then said, "Tell me, my son, you seem to be well versed in our teachings. Tell us about Heaven. What is it like?

Like a chain reaction, those who heard the question chimed in, "Yes, tell us. What is it like? Tell us, please tell us."

Elijah looked at the priest and asked, "What is Heaven and what is hell?"

Father Owens responded, "Heaven, as we all know, is a place where God's children will meet with Him in glory. And hell is a place where sinners will burn for eternity."

"And how do you know this to be true?"

"I know this to be the truth because I am a man of the cloth and it is my business to know the words of God."

"Is it possible that our Heavenly Father has made the truth with many doors in order to welcome anyone who knocks on them?"

"I do not understand."

"In your teaching, is there any room for another truth?"

"I suppose so, but tell us, young man, what is your truth?"

Elijah got up and looked at the people who were waiting anxiously for his words as they still tried to understand why his voice sounded so clear as it reached their hearts, no matter how far away they were. They could hear him as if they were close enough to touch his garments.

"If you think hell is a place where you will burn throughout eternity, then you are wrong. If you think Heaven is above and hell is below, then you are surely wrong."

His audience was quiet; the sound of a pin could have been heard miles away should one have fallen to the ground. And as he continued, they listened intensely to what some viewed as the most unusual perception of Heaven and hell they had ever heard.

"I say this unto you, my fellow brethren, that hell does not exist, and Heaven is more than just a place. It's a feeling, a feeling that comes with being one with the holy light of God. It is the fulfillment of merging your soul with God's. When we speak of mansions, we speak of the multitude of religious ideologies that allow man to unite himself with God. This is the embodiment of my Father's kingdom."

Father Owens became annoyed at what Elijah had said. "The Bible teaches us of hell; to choose one is to reject the other."

"Old man, what has to be done in order to enter the Father's kingdom? Tell me."

"That's easy. Obey the Ten Commandments, live your life in accordance with the Scriptures, and do only good."

"But have you done only good deeds all your life? For is it not so that all have sinned and fallen short of the glory of God?"

"Yes, but doing good deeds, worshipping and praising God, and loving one another, these are the true criteria for getting to Heaven."

"You strive to do good always, but do you?"

"No!"

"Have you ever sinned against man and the Heavenly Father?"

"Sure I have. As you just said, all have sinned and fallen short of the glory of God, so I am no exception to the rule."

"Indeed you are not. And neither are all these people or any member of the human race. I tell you this, old man, that when you leave this Earth, you must answer for the bad and evil side of you as sure as you will be reinforced and glorified for the good and wonderful side of you. But hell will not be a part of my Father's system of judgement. For any man who enters into my Father's kingdom must think not of a place down, for it does not exist. In my father's kingdom there are two doors, one on the right and one on the left. Each man must enter the door on the left and pay atonement for all his sins, his evil ways, and the deeds that were not in accordance with my Father's teachings and expectations. If the man is beyond redemption, he will simply cease to exist. If he is one with the spirit of the Messiah, he will join the holy circle or be placed back in a woman's womb. This is a room of judgement. If he finds redemption and seeks not to be placed back in a woman's womb or is reluctant to rejoin the holy circle, then the third option will be to enter the door on the right where he can elect to stay in one of the many compartments and live out his perception of Heaven and concept of pleasure throughout eternity."

Father Owens interrupted Elijah. "So are you telling us and asking us to believe that in the case of a perverted individual who acquires pleasure only from sexual means, his heaven will be a total maximization of his sexual wishes? Are you asking us to believe that Heaven will be fulfilling this man's desires, wishes, and fantasies?"

Elijah was quiet then he responded simply, "Yes, if God granted him redemption." Elijah's response sent the crowd into a frenzy as people became alarmed at what he had just said. Elijah then spoke again. "Old man, do you like ice cream?"

"Yes, who doesn't?"

"What's your favorite flavor?"

"Chocolate. I love chocolate."

"Old man, as you know no pleasure is universal, for pleasure is relative to each individual. Hence why should everyone be subjected to the same things that give them a heavenly feeling when each individual finds pleasure in different things. If a man wants to achieve pleasure from violence and killing, then his wish will be granted. He will be allowed to roam with others like himself who seek pleasure from killing others and they will fight and kill one another through eternity. They will enjoy it, and they will play their games, for they can no longer die; they will be immortal and in their immortality they will do the things that give them pleasure forever and ever. To the man who loves sex and achieves pleasure from things pertaining to that nature, his pleasure will be maximized and he will be allowed to move amongst others who fit the same category. Throughout eternity they will explode in passion and live in a life of pleasure over and over. Heaven, old man, is the maximization of one's ultimate pleasure and desires. Yes, old man, whether you believe it or not, contrary to your teachings, Heaven and God are one and there is no hell. The darkest region of man's mind and man's inner soul, the evil that dwells within them, this is the bottomless pit, and not the hole in which man shall be cast and burn throughout eternity. This is not my Father's way, rather it is only a delusion that man suffers."

"Yes, young man. But didn't Jesus go to the bottom of the pit, the pits of hell when he died? Isn't there some truth to this scenario?"

"In my father's death he came to know his inner evil, which all men possess; he has mastered the darkest regions of our mind and in doing so he has come to be the master not only of Heaven but also of man's imperfections, not as you insist it to be but as I know it to be."

"You are an extraordinary young man with an unorthodox way of thinking about our teachings. I only hope that this way of thinking will not one day get you into trouble."

"It already has," replied Elijah as he walked away. In the midst of the crowd, the people shook Elijah's hand as he walked by. Though he could tell from their eyes and their hearts that some did not believe some of the things he had said, he knew they meant well. Elijah walked amongst the crowd and almost stumbled over the feet of a Korean man who seemed distraught. Looking directly into the man's eyes, he said, "Sometimes the answer is 'no.' "

The man did not acknowledge Elijah's statement immediately but after a while replied, "She's the only thing I ever wanted. Now the day before our wedding I find out she is not a virgin. Why would God deny me the only woman I have ever loved?" asked the Korean man, who identified himself as Sang Li.

"God did not deny you your bride; you have denied yourself."

"But how can I accept her when she is not a virgin? In my country a woman must remain pure until the day of her wedding."

"There is no such thing as virginity amongst women. How can this be when there is no purity within conception? For each woman was molested at the time she was conceived by her mother. Hence every woman's father carries a heavy burden on his shoulders."

"Are you saying that a woman who has never had a sexual experience of any kind is still not a virgin?" asked Sang Li.

"Yes."

"But why not?"

"Because the process by which she came into being has already engaged her in a sexual encounter with her father, with the sperm that runs from his body. Hence, this is why our heavenly Father had chosen an immaculate conception in order to enter my father into this world over two thousand years ago."

"But my friends and family, what will they think when they find out she is not a virgin? I don't think I can handle the gossip."

"Gossips are empty words that lose their identity in the face of truth."

"You mean I should tell them."

"Yes."

Sang Li hung his head as he pondered what Elijah had said. Then he asked, "Why am I not content?"

"Because you are not at peace with yourself and the entities of the universe."

"I would like to be but I don't know how."

"Embrace the elements of the universe by allowing them to become a part of you, since you're not already a part of them. When it comes to relationship, Sang Li, there are two types of men. One can be sensitive and emotional, but his heart operates only under the guidelines of his libido or hormones. The other is a type of man who can also be sensitive, warm, and kind, but his heart does not operate without the benefit of his intellect. By knowing which one you are, you can pretty much know why you're not able to forgive your potential bride."

"I feel like the respect I once had for her has died."

"How can you kill something that never existed? But if your respect for her has died, as you claim, then find yourself another bride." Elijah started to walk away.

"But I still love her. Why should I find myself another bride?"

"Because the extent of your love is based on a tradition that still holds you captive. So find another bride, but before you do get yourself a bucket of clay."

"Why do I need a bucket of clay?"

"So you can mold yourself a woman, one who is without sin," replied Elijah as he continued to walk amongst the crowd.

A few minutes later Elijah heard a question ring out from the crowd. "Is God pro-choice or pro-life?"

"When life is aborted, it is God's way of redirecting a gift to someone more deserving or more able. He is neither pro-choice nor pro-life, for man cannot dictate to God when an entity should or should not come into being."

Elijah continued to walk, then he heard another question that had a twist of humor to it. "Do you think our political system is the best in the world?"

"I will answer that question by reciting a poem that one of my teachers taught me:

"They sit in judgement in a political arena
As they set forth the hierarchy by which we live.
They have become spectators to a political entity
That lacks consciousness in any true sense of awareness.
They dominate through total dictatorship
That disguises itself in the form of democracy.
They are gods, the rulers.

They would have us sacrifice ourselves
For the price of liberty,
When behind closed doors
They acknowledge that the fight
Is indeed for their own salvation.

They do not promote peace with trust and love,
Rather with strength behind arms.
They do not sing and rejoice
In the name of one God,
Rather in the name of themselves—
For they have become gods.

Now their walls of delusion are coming down,
For there is conflict in Babylon,
A volcano in Heaven,
And turmoil amongst the gods.

What will they do?
How will they react
Now that they are plagued
With pestilence and diseases beyond their control?
Who will fulfill the prophesy
And be one amongst men?
For is it not so
That a true leader will die for his people?
Yet we are asked to die for our leaders.

Death comes in many forms
But true love only in one."

After a while, Elijah was tired and invited the crowd to come another day.

23

Before Elijah left the Monument grounds, a man, slender in stature, approached him. The man appeared confused. He touched Elijah on the hand, then immediately stepped away. "Hi. You have a minute?" asked what seemed to be a very quiet and introverted man.

Elijah looked at the man, who seemed to be in his mid-30s, and knew fate had dealt the man a losing hand. "Sure."

"I've been listening to you and I am just a little curious about something, that's all."

"About what?"

"You see, I have this illness. Doctors don't have a cure, you know, and I, well, I was kinda wondering what would happen if I take my own life. My pastor said no one goes to Heaven if they commit suicide. Is there any truth to that?"

"What is your name?"

"Lewin. My friends call me Lee."

"Are you a Christian, Lee?"

"Yes, I am. I go to a Pentecostal church."

"When the gift of life becomes a burden, where it is no longer considered a gift to an individual, then it is not wrong to return it from where it came."

"My pastor said life is precious and no one but God has the right to take it; rather, it should be guarded at all cost. But now you are saying it is alright?"

"Life is for living, and if this is prohibited by any factor or means, then it becomes life under siege. When life is imprisoned by circumstances, the prospect of death can be a salvation within itself."

"But is it not a sin to take your own life?"

"If this is so then my father, who represents the closest thing to perfection, would have sinned, and he is without sin."

"I do not understand. Why would he have sinned?"

"I will answer your question by first asking you one. If you know that when you leave and go to that store across the street a man would take your life, would you go across the street?"

"No, that would be insane."

"But if you did, would you consider your action an act of suicide?"

"Yes."

"Why?"

"Because I would know death awaited me, yet I would willingly allow it to happen."

"Now, do you think my father the Messiah had a choice with his death?"

"I don't know. What do you mean?"

"Did he have free will as we all do to say yes or no to dying for the sins of humanity?"

"Sure, he was the son of God. He could have said no, but he knew dying was his purpose for coming on this Earth."

"Regardless of why he died, he knew death awaited him, yet he gladly allowed himself to be sacrificed. Now I ask you, is this gesture an act of suicide?"

"It sounds like it."

"When my father said, 'it is finished' on the cross, it was his way of saying 'my life has become burdensome, for on my shoulders rest the burden of the entire world. Now I return it to you for it is no longer a gift that will allow me to live in a way to which I have grown accustomed.' "

"So you are saying that Christ committed suicide?"

"Yes! There is always a reason to die, sometimes even if it means going against the schedule of the angel of death. No! My father will not close his doors on those who have felt the need to hasten death, not for reasons that he can understand."

Lee looked at Elijah and thanked him for talking to him. Before Lee walked away, Elijah saw that Lee was troubled and that he had the opportunity to extinguish his interpersonal conflicts. "Whatever I can do to make your load lighter, I will do," he said.

"I don't want to go to Heaven," said Lee firmly.

"Do you not think yourself worthy?"

"That's the problem."

"Now I am confused."

"All my life I have been subjected to racism, prejudice, and the ugliness of others. People do it to me in subtle ways; other times it is as blatant as the nose on my face. Some of these people call themselves Christians, God-loving people. I tell you, man, I have this disease that is killing me, but when I die I'm sure I don't want to go to Heaven if people like that will be there. I am sick and tired of being a Black man in this country. Every goddamn thing that is associated with 'black' seems to be negative in this country. Dying may be a blessed thing after all. Maybe I will come back as a white man and run for the presidency."

Elijah stood there and listened, knowing that Lee was on the verge of tears. Then, as if he had missed everything that Lee had said, Elijah burst out in laughter. Lee was startled by Elijah's reaction. 'I am glad to see that one of us can still laugh about being a Black man in this society."

Elijah tried to compose himself, started to speak, but ended up in uncontrollable laughter once again.

"You think I am joking. Someone dies, what do you wear: a black dress. Even plague is goddamn black."

"Open your eyes and come out of the light. Be one with the darkness. Allow it to lead you to the path of inner peace."

"What do you mean?"

"You're so consumed with the negative things that are associated with Blacks and the stigma that goes with them that you have neglected the wonderful things that come with the same color. You talked about wearing a black dress at the time of death as if it degrades the color black. You fail to understand that true life begins with death, which makes any color that is a part of that process a color of which to be proud. The most sanctified and holy words that have ever been written by men inspired by God are entrusted and clothed by the color of darkness."

"The Bible. You mean the Bible, don't you?"

"Yes. But the irony of your concerns is that in my Father's kingdom, the very colors of man's skin that pit them against one another in a struggle for racial superiority, in essence, will be the very dimension that will bind them together."

"You have lost me," Lee responded.

"Be assured that you will find harmony in my Father's kingdom."

"But don't they have Black, white, Chinese, and other skin colors up there?"

"No."

"You mean everybody will be made into white?"

"You will be an entity, an energy that illuminates beautiful colors that are presently beyond man's comprehension or imagination. The majestic beauty and delight of this coloring will keep you intrigued with the content of your being forever. There will be no time for man's idiotic idiosyncrasies for the mystery of his very existence will keep him perturbed and fascinated throughout eternity. This will be less than a fraction of the things that will keep your mind wondering. No, my brother, in my Father's kingdom the color you will see will bring men together, not divide them."

Lee hung his head, then walked up closer to Elijah, hugged him tightly, and said, "Take care of yourself, if I don't see you again."

"But you will, and yes, I am aware of man's reluctance to accept the son of man being of dark skin. I see it in their paintings on the street, and even in the churches that still try to deny this fact by replacing portraits of my father's 'blonde' hair with wooden statues. For this is their compromise to giving credit where it is due."

Suddenly Lee stopped and Elijah could see that Lee's mind was still not at ease. "Are you really the son of Jesus?"

"What do you think?"

"Well, there is no mention of you in the Bible."

"That still does not answer my question."

"I suppose anything is possible, but I really don't know. You seem to know a lot, but a lot of people say you're gifted and that it is getting to your head. You must admit that going around telling people that you are the son of God is a little bit much."

"I did not claim to be the son of God."

"Yes, you did."

"No, my claim was that of the son of the Messiah."

"Oh, but isn't Jesus also God? They are the same, aren't they?"

"No."

"What do you mean, no? Reverend Townsend told me that God is the Father, God is the son, and God is the holy ghost. He said that God has three different personalities. Jesus is God and God is Jesus."

"To say that God has three different personalities would give birth to the idea that the heavenly Father has a multiple personality disorder. The heavenly Father has no psychopathologies."

"But if Jesus was not God, who was he?"

"Simply the son of God, as stated over and over in various versions of your Bible. In my Father's house are many mansions; for God so loved the world that he sent his only begotten son; no man cometh unto the Father but by me; *eli, eli, lama sabathani.* It goes on and on, yet man refuses to accept that the Father, son, and holy ghost are three different entities."

"Didn't Jesus himself say, 'I and my Father are one'?"

"Yes."

"Then isn't he saying that he is God and God is he?"

"No. Do you have any children?"

"Yes, one boy."

"You're the father, he's the son, and one day you may have a grandchild. This makes all three of you separate entities. Still you are one because the blood that runs through your veins runs through theirs, making you a part of one another. Hence three different entities linked together as one by blood.

Such is the holy trinity; three separate entities with individualized personalities linked together as one by a spiritual connection. I say it and I'll say it again, the heavenly Father cannot look at sin. This is why the Messiah was sent, that through him man may cleanse himself by his deeds, his faith, and his love. It is only by this cleansing will man find himself in the presence of God."

"I really enjoy talking to you, Elijah. I hope you're for real because a lot of people believe in you."

"How could my vision be blurred by the onset of corruption when my blood is that of the Messiah?" Lee started to walk away but Elijah stopped him. "Remember, Lewin, if the process of thinking cannot change a situation, then it is unwise to influence the mind to that which may cause harm to the body." They both went their separate ways as Elijah realized that he was late for an important meeting.

24

In preparation for Elijah's arrival, the members of the Nation of Islam set up a panel of their brightest dignitaries to discuss some of Elijah's teachings. This meeting would also serve as a format to voice their concerns about the effect Elijah was having on people, mainly the young Black men who had begun turning away from the teachings of Islam to what they considered the radical and fanatical aspirations of an untamed man.

Twelve men assembled in a large room, passing the coffeepot back and forth to one another as they stared at the empty chair complemented by its matching antique table. The men were dressed in expensive suits and bow ties; the Rolexes and Bertolluccis on their hands epitomized their economic status. They engaged in idle chatter while awaiting their guest, who was by now late in arriving for his scheduled meeting.

Half an hour went by and Haleem, a heavyset man who was seated in the middle of the panel, pounded his fist on the table and said to a colleague on his far left, "Ali, are you sure today is the day he said he would be here?"

"Yes, that's what Brother Hakeem told me," replied Ali.

"You mean Brother Hakeem set this entire thing up?"

"Yes."

"No wonder. Hell, we might as well all go home."

Before another word could be said, the squeaking of the door echoed in the room and the sound brought with it a young man who stood before them in worn-out jeans and a long white shirt, which was worn outside the pants. He was not wearing any shoes. As he slowly walked toward the men, Ali said, "You have the wrong room, pal." But the young man kept walking toward them and before long they could clearly see the face of Elijah, who now stood before them in silence.

"He looks like a homeless person," whispered Haleem to Fattaah, who was seated directly beside him.

"Until a man finds security within the presence of my Father, we are all homeless," responded Elijah.

Haleem was shocked that Elijah had heard his whisper. "No offense intended Elijah," he said, "just a little humor."

Elijah turned about and walked over to the table and chair that were obviously set out for his convenience. He picked up the chair and put it aside, sat on the table in his usual lotus position, then looked at the twelve men.

"Well, as long as you are comfortable. . . ." said Brother Haleem. Elijah did not respond.

"We are glad you decided to join us, brother. We have heard great things about you, things that only a man who has been touched by Allah could have done. We are baffled, nevertheless, why you choose to proclaim yourself the son of the Messiah. Why, after two thousand years, would an alleged son of the Messiah finally decide to return and live amongst us? Tell me this, brother, why?" asked Haleem, who apparently was the spokesperson for his colleagues.

Elijah was quiet and his silence took the focus from him and placed it on them.

"Are you with us?" asked Brother Ali.

"I have never left; now my presence serves a purpose," said Elijah.

"And what is this purpose?" asked Brother Haleem.

"To help you find the things you have lost within the simplicity of its meaning."

"And what are these things?" asked Brother Haleem.

"Love, respect, and racial harmony," said Elijah.

"Indeed, these values we hold dear, to love and respect our brothers and to strive for racial harmony," replied Brother Haleem.

"When I talk to my brothers of Islam, their words are empty, filled with anger; their hearts are filled with mixed emotions; they do not know whether to love or hate the white man. Their minds are confused, caught between the values they were once taught by their parents and the ones you breathe into them. No! You do not strive for racial harmony but for racial separation. The only distinction between you and the white man in this regard is that he does not camouflage his intent to obtain and maintain racial superiority behind any empty search for racial equality," said Elijah.

"Who the hell are you to speak to us this way?" shouted Brother Ali angrily.

"We're instilling pride and Black consciousness in our young brothers and sisters. We, too, would like racial harmony but this will never exist, not in this society. For in the eyes of the white man we'll always be lesser than they," said Brother Haleem.

"How long will you live your lives through the eyes of the white man and not through the eyes of God? In your zealousness to separate yourselves from the white man, you have separated yourselves from yourselves and from God," said Elijah.

"What do you mean?" asked Brother Haleem.

"You seldom see the goodness of things if it is a part of the white structure, and when you do see them, envy, jealousy, and rage spark within your heart, for you feel cheated out of the things the white man possesses. I ask you, is it that you hate the white man or you wish you were like him?"

"We do not need to be like the white man. We're from a generation of kings and queens; we are proud to be Black," said Brother Haleem.

"A race as ours that has so much pride should not find the need to struggle so hard for acceptance of its own identity. This is our Father's kingdom," said Elijah.

"You tell *them* that. They think they own the whole goddamn world," said Ali.

"If they do, it is only because you have given them the avenue to do so," replied Elijah, who closed his eyes for a moment or two then opened them quickly and said, "Glory be to God for his kindness and mercy far exceed our worthiness."

They watched him as he slowly emerged from what appeared to have been a hypnotic trance.

"You're not a spiritual man, Elijah; you're an intellectual. Intellectualism must always be placed secondary to spiritualism. If you were truly sent by Allah, you would have conducted yourself differently today," said Ali.

Elijah held his head down for a minute as the twelve men gazed at one another. Then he spoke: "Wisdom is the offspring of experience, but intelligence is the foundation for wisdom. If intelligence were a barrier to secure man's faith in God, why then did God give man intelligence? Why then did he choose the three wise men to seek out the birthplace of my father? Is not being omniscient the epitome of intelligence and wisdom, which is the embodiment of God? No, my brothers, intelligence must never be placed secondary to spiritualism, for you cannot find one without the other."

"We do not want you to lead the young Black men of this society astray. The notion of being humble and waiting for the white man to give you scrap went out with the eighteenth century. It's all about being strong and taking back what is rightfully ours," said Brother Haleem.

"Strength begins with humility. All things belong to God. Until man realizes that the worldly possessions he holds are as elusive as the wind, he will never truly understand the futility of his constant struggle to be a part of the Earth."

"It is not about owning a part of the Earth, Elijah. It is about living on it with a degree of comfort. Why are you so blind to the oppression of our people?" asked Haleem.

"Yes, I am blind and even disturbed, but not by the oppression that plagues our people," replied Elijah.

"Then by what?" asked Brother Haleem.

"By the hypocrisy and the mask that are often used to justify your good intent," said Elijah.

"Do we have to listen to this garbage?" asked Brother Ali angrily.

"No," responded Elijah as he got up from the table and started to walk toward the door.

"Please, Brother Ali, control yourself. Do not leave, Elijah, please," said Brother Haleem.

Elijah went back and seated himself on the table. Tension was still in the air, but Elijah continued.

"It is not my intent to take away the good you have done, only to illuminate the inconsistencies that have often cast a shadow on the meaningfulness behind your gesture. When the KKK marches and emphasizes racial purity and superiority, such an act is viewed as grotesque by our people. When I listen to the members of Islam, the content of their speech stresses the doctrine of anti-white. If you find the need to promulgate a religious doctrine merely because it is anti-white, then do so with honor so God and the men can be proud. I see no difference between the message from the Nation of Islam and the message from the KKK. If the foundation of both messages is love and respect toward humanity, then yes, I must be blind, for I do not see this."

"Surely you cannot compare the Nation of Islam to the KKK," said Brother Haleem.

Elijah was slow to respond. "I do not; your messages do."

"Sometimes we must fight fire with fire," said Brother Haleem.

"A man who casts himself into the lion's den to convince himself and others that he is not afraid of the lion is guilty not of courage but of stupidity. I say fight fire not with fire but with love, for the heat of a towering inferno will cease to give heat in the presence of true love," said Elijah.

"Sometimes to empower young people, we must first point out the injustices and unfairness of the society in which they live," said Brother Haleem.

"If the principles of Allah and the righteousness of the Messiah are not enough to empower them, then the conditioning of human frailties cannot," said Elijah.

"So what do you suggest we do when we are slapped in the face by the white man? Turn the other cheek?" asked Brother Ali in his usual arrogant way.

Elijah looked at the other members of the panel, who were pensive in their silence, then he responded to Brother Ali's question. "No. Do not turn the other cheek; rather, offer them the same one. A man's conscience is a reflection of his soul. The white man may not understand a lot of things about our people, but they do have souls. After a while they will come to realize that the disrespect and the hate they feel toward our people is eating away at their souls like a parasite. His guilt will weigh heavily on his conscience and this will be the beginning of the end."

"I understand your words, Elijah. But it is only fair that we fight back against their unfairness," said Brother Haleem.

"Yes, but with a sword in one hand and love in the other, not hate," replied Elijah.

"Thanks for coming. At least we are sure that Allah did not send you to us," said Ali sarcastically.

"You are out of line, Brother Ali. We invited Elijah here. We may not share his views but we must respect them," interjected Brother Haleem. He then turned to Elijah and said, "We sincerely applaud you for coming, Elijah. What final message do you have for us?"

Elijah looked at each panel member, one by one, then when he got to Brother Ali he focused on him and said, "Do not worry, but if you must, then worry by necessity. When I see Brother Ali, I see a man who worries about how society is structured, the unfairness it shows toward our people; a man who worries about keeping up or surpassing the white man; a man who worries about keeping what he has obtained from this predominantly white society, and on and on. His worries will never stop."

"You got that right. Got to always keep a step ahead of the white man," said Brother Ali.

"Indeed, but when do you live?" Elijah asked.

"Live? Man, that's my life," replied Brother Ali.

"It's a pity then, for it is a wasted one," responded Elijah who closed his eyes as Brother Ali became annoyed once again, which was evident from some of his remarks and criticisms.

Ali continued to ramble on. This time not even Brother Haleem could control the verbal abuse.

The table on which Elijah was sitting suddenly started to lift itself from its four legs and sailed him through the air like a magic carpet, acting as if it had a mind of its own. It gently placed Elijah midway of the path to the door through which he had arrived. Seconds later, the tabletop returned to its legs as if nothing had interrupted the work of some carpenter's masterpiece.

Meanwhile, the members of the panel sat in astonishment. Brother Ali grabbed his throat after realizing that his vocal cords were not allowing him to project any sound from his mouth.

"A talker can seldom hear the voice of an angel because he is made deaf by his own baffling sound," said Elijah. By now all twelve members of the panel were on their feet watching Elijah as he slowly walked toward the door. They noticed that at every step he made, his feet were greeted with what appeared to be red sand. Not once did his bare feet touch the ground. As he opened the door, he turned around and said, "As Salaamu' Alaikum wa Rahmatullaah," then disappeared, leaving them standing with their thoughts.

25

While a humble divinity walked the land, the president was masterminding his own agenda. Passions erupted, creating a heat within his hormones as he sought an outlet by embracing the ideation of having a bodily encounter. Overwhelmed with the anticipation of engulfing the excitement of his woman's physique, the commander-in-chief roared at his servants. "Damn it, Wilson, can't you go any faster?"

"Sorry sir, but traffic is a little hectic."

The president looked at his watch and uttered beneath his breath, "Next time I am getting an official escort; to hell with the taxpayers!"

Twenty minutes later the president arrived at his destination. Before leaving the car, he glanced at Wilson and Frederick, then asked, "Where am I, boys?"

"Walter Reed, sir," replied both Secret Service agents simultaneously. They watched him as he took what appeared to be an overnight bag and went into a beach house.

"I don't know where he gets his energy from. He's fifty-two years old and he's still acting like a wild stallion," Wilson said.

"You don't suppose he's going through a midlife crisis, do you?" Frederick asked.

"Hell, I have been driving him since he was governor. He has always been like this. So whatever he is going through, I wouldn't mind going through it with whomever he meets inside that house every Thursday night."

"You don't think he would invite us up as standby, just in case his back goes out, do you?" Frederick laughed.

"Hell, no. It's 9:00 P.M., what do you say we go and have a few drinks?"

"Sounds good. At least we have the rest of the night off."

"Bet you would still like to have some of what he's going to get tonight, though, wouldn't you?"

"Hell, yes," replied Frederick as they drove away from the front of the isolated house on the beach. Using the two men as an alibi, the president soon found himself on his way to Peterson's home. Dressed like a blonde, driving an unmarked car he prepared for his evil deed.

Later on that night, Peterson and his wife copulated, and as he tried to go beyond her vaginal wall with his penis, his counterpart screamed as she moved her body erotically on him like a wild horse being broken by a cowboy. Lying on his back with only the mattress on the floor, he glimpsed at their reflections in the ceiling mirror as both ends of the long nylon cord around their necks slid on the iron bar. Each multiorgasmic climax intensified the extravaganza resulting in the pulling of the nylon cord, creating an aroma which derives from a moment of ecstacy that literally left both partners breathless as they indulged in sexual hypoxia.

Seized as prisoners of their own pleasure, blinded by the ecstacy and the explosion of their hormones, they didn't notice the intruder who stood in the shadow watching every move. Peterson lay with his eyes closed, reliving the sexual experience in his mind, as his wife flashed her hair back, refusing to cause a separation of the two genitals. A smile came on her face as she felt the nylon cord take on a life of its own and began to slowly put her in a state of asphyxiation, allowing her to explore her libido energy in a world that lies between the conscious and unconscious without crossing the boundary that would lead to payment of the ultimate price.

She tapped her fingers on Peterson's legs, a signal that normally warned him when he should loosen his grip on the nylon cord. She panicked as he ignored the signal that could mean the difference between life and death, not knowing that he was totally unaware of what was happening. She tried to scream, but before a sound could leave her throat, a pair of hands yanked her to the ceiling, hanging her with the nylon cord.

Disturbed by the sudden jerk that almost broke his own neck, Peterson opened his eyes to see his wife strung up on the iron rod in the ceiling. Before he could get up, she came crashing to the floor. Half of her body landed on the mattress and the other half on the bare floor. Seconds later, as he attempted to crawl like a baby over to her side, he noticed a gun pointed to his head.

"See what happens when you screw things up?" said the voice.

Peterson slowly turned around to face the man who within a split second had taken away from him the only woman he had ever loved. "You! You'll never get away with it," he screamed.

"Hell, I'm the president. I've already gotten away with it," replied the president as he pulled the other end of the nylon cord, sending Peterson to the ceiling, kicking and gasping for air. The president held the cord for a moment, making sure that Peterson was dead. He then relaxed his grip, allowing Peterson to hit the floor. Blood gushed from Peterson's head.

On his way out, he muttered to himself, "I should have known better than to send a drunk to do a man's job."

26

Three days after the death of Peterson and his wife, Father Andreas found himself relishing the zenith of the occurrences of what he thought had led to the fate of Elijah. In preparation for that Sunday's rituals, he was the first to enter the church in order to ensure a positive impression from his congregation. Enmeshed in his superficial attributes, he no longer saw God as an authority of good and bad whose guidance he needed, but rather as an obstacle that stood in the way of his ambition and lust for power.

Singing at the top of his voice an old familiar hymn, he took out a match to light the two candles that were on opposite sides of the altar. He lit the one on the right first, then walked over to light the other. He tried to light the candle but the match went out. Realizing that was his last matchstick, he took a piece of paper, held it over the already lit candle, then hurried to the other side, attempting to light the other candle again. Suddenly the flame ignited the candle, creating an explosion of fire that engulfed Father Andreas and nearby objects.

Within minutes fire trucks were on the scene as they attempted to bring a halt to the fiery inferno. A lady screamed, "Look, someone is on the balcony!" as the blaze from the fire stretched its ugly head, trying to take the life of an elderly man next door who appeared to be in his late eighties.

The man watched as the church next to him continued to burn out of control. He then grabbed his walking stick and made tiny steps back inside the house. Minutes later he made tiny steps back to the balcony with a small cup of water in his hands. Face to face with the flames, like a dragonslayer facing a dragon, he threw the cup of water at the flames while other neighbors were jumping over one another trying to escape the fire. The elderly man slowly went back into the house, as the onlookers breathed a sigh of relief thinking that now he too would make his escape before the fire spread to his house. But out he came again with another cup of water in his hand, and again threw the water at the flames. Before he could go back inside the house, a fireman got to him and threw the old man over his shoulders, carrying him to safety.

Meanwhile, back at the White House, the president watched the entire incident on TV. "Forgive me Father, for I know not what I do," said the president with a grin.

"Did you say something, dear?" asked the First Lady.

"No, everything is just fine."

27

The next morning after the deliberate torching of St. Margaret's Church, Dr. Weinstein woke up at his residence. Still in a twilight-like sleep, he held his aching head and tried to swallow, realizing that his mouth was unusually dry. He attributed his fatigue and restlessness to insomnia, totally disregarding what appeared to have been a nightmare in which he was held down and drugged by a man dressed in full black with a stocking over his head.

Weinstein slowly removed the sheet from on top of him and tried to get out of bed. His movements triggered a sophisticated bomb that was strapped to his chest. Each time he tried to move, the device on his chest set off a beeping sound that became louder and also moved the hand on the clock from the white closer to the red mark. Weinstein started to panic. Perspiration dripped off his eyebrows. "Please God, no," he said as he realized that though he was not now moving, the tone of the beep was still becoming louder and the hand was still moving closer toward the red mark.

"No," he said once again. This time he realized that the sound of his voice had desensitized the bomb, stabilizing it to the point where the beeping tone had decreased and the hand was slowly returning to the white mark. "Is the patient ready?" he asked, trying to reassure himself of his observations. A smile came on his face as his suspicions were confirmed.

Weinstein started to sing, "London Bridge is falling down, my fair lady," while trying to move toward the phone. The bomb became unstable once again, so he quickly relaxed himself back in the bed. His voice began to crack as he sang aloud, "London Bridge is falling down, falling down, falling down."

Minutes later the bomb's tone and dial were at an equilibrium once again.

Two hours went by and Weinstein became tired of hearing himself sing "London Bridge" as a new sound emerged from his vocal cords. "Ninety-nine bottles of beer on the wall, ninety-nine bottles of beer. If one of those bottles should happen to fall, . . ." His voice continued to soothe the temperamental device planted on his chest, like a mother's breast stopping an infant's crying.

Another two hours went by and Weinstein's mouth had become as dry as the Sahara Desert. By this time his anguish had made him regress even to the point where he was recollecting many more of his childhood favorites. "Little Bo Peep has lost her sheep, and doesn't know where to find them. Leave them alone and they will come home . . ." He burst out in tears as he looked across the night table and saw the picture of his seven-year-old daughter Andrea and his wife, who were living only a few miles from him.

Weinstein's sadness turned into laughter as he focused only on his wife. "You always said I don't talk; now look at me, you can't shut me up. One of life's many ironies." Seized by the bomb strapped to his chest, accepting the inevitable outcome that fate had placed him in, he whispered softly beneath his breath, "Forgive me, Elijah." He closed his eyes as a big and peaceful smile came over his face. His silence sent the hand on the bomb to the red mark. Seconds later he was one with the brotherhood of death as his silence triggered a massive explosion.

28

A few weeks later Elijah received a letter from the pope inviting him to return to Rome. The invitation gave the impression that there was an emergency but did not specify what it was. Elijah accepted the invitation and soon found himself at the Vatican.

That evening the pope greeted Elijah with a worried look on his face. Since it was late in the evening, the Pope suggested that Elijah rest from his long journey and they would talk first thing the next morning. Although Elijah tried to tell the pope that he was not tired and that it was alright, he finally accommodated the pope by yielding to his suggestions. The pope made sure that his servants were at Elijah's beck and call.

Elijah was far more tired than he'd thought, because as soon as he hit the bed he was out like a light. He was awakened several hours later by a strange sound in his room. He could not see anything but he knew he had heard something. Suddenly he saw a shadow in the dark, a faceless man, it would appear. Silence had taken over the room, for neither Elijah nor the individual whom the shadow belonged to was saying anything.

A few minutes passed, then Elijah spoke, "Be aware of a man who hides his true intention behind flowery words of praise and polite conversation, for he is like a woman who hides her ugliness with cosmetics."

Elijah's words sent the owner of the shadow closer to the light. First the hand could be seen through the dimness of the light. The reflection from the moon cast a shadow on a gun that was pointed toward Elijah. Elijah was not concerned. There was more silence.

"Even Judas had the courage to betray his master with a kiss, for even he realized that those that prey at night will be accused by day by the stains of the blood," Elijah continued.

The person came closer to Elijah so his face and entire image could be seen. The pope saw that Elijah was not surprised. Elijah looked at him and said, "The time has come."

"You do not seem surprised, young man. I hope you will understand that this is nothing personal. I agree with some of the things you have said, but most of them I do not. You do not speak the whole truth. God would never agree with some of the things you've been saying. Thanks to my brethren, I learned this in time."

"I may possess my father's eyes and even a part of his soul, but my ability to reason will sometimes keep us separate."

"That may be so, but the Catholic truth is more than just a doctrine or a way of life. It is a business and we can't have you going around with your popularity speaking things that are not in accord with our teachings. So Father Andropolus, the other members of the staff, and myself decided to end it once and for all so people can focus their attention on the Catholic way of life and teaching. You do understand that this is nothing personal, don't you, young man? This is only business."

"When a caterpillar refuses to change into a butterfly, it's usually for a good reason. Indeed, some people seek pleasure in pain while others cannot cleanse themselves except with filth."

"You must understand, young man, that I wanted to make this easier on both of us by doing it while you were sleeping, but I stumbled; that's what woke you up. I am sorry I did that, but it is now a little more difficult than I imagined."

"Breaking the law of God is never easy, but I understand. When a man must make a decision that involves choosing between his sense of justice and his sense of loyalty, there can be no right decision, for either way he will become a traitor to himself. Still, he must choose." Elijah then closed his eyes and recited an old familiar verse that was used by his father two thousand years ago. "Father, in thy hands I commit my spirit, for it is now up to them to choose between what I have said and what you have taught them. Forgive them for the things they do in your name."

Before Elijah could open his mouth to say another word, the gun went off, sending a bullet into his head. As Elijah lay on his back with his brains splashed all over the floor, the pope looked at him and just to make sure he was dead, fired another shot into Elijah's head. The pope then left the room. A few minutes after the deed was done, several men came in dressed in army uniforms, put Elijah's body in a bag, cleaned up the room, and carried him away.

Later on that morning, a time when the sun was usually out, it was not, and people began to wonder why this was the case because the land was once again swept by complete darkness. People all over the world were frightened at this phenomenon and although they tried to explain it they could not. The Vatican and the White House knew that they had committed the ultimate sin once again against God as the Romans, the Pharisees, and the Jews did two thousand years ago. Still, forgiveness was the theme of Elijah's death as the heavenly Father paid tribute to his son by keeping the Earth in darkness for two days.

EPILOGUE

Three days later Elijah's murder was blamed on an unknown assailant who had no apparent motive. Although Elijah was killed in Rome, his body was discovered in an alley in Washington, D.C., by a member of the Salvation Army, who recognized him right away. News of his death spread rapidly, as was evident by the international coverage it received. Even the pope in Rome held a special mass in Elijah's honor, while in the United States, the president interrupted all the local news channels just to tell the public how saddened he was by Elijah's death. The president's speech on Elijah's death quickly deviated to several campaign promises. The world mourned a great loss, even though many did not believe that Elijah was the son of the Messiah. Still, they knew he represented good, which was evident by his miracles and his understanding of the human heart.

On the day of Elijah's funeral, the president, the pope, and the head of the AME Zion Church were among his pallbearers. Dignitaries from all over the world came to pay tribute to a young man who had touched their hearts in one way or another.

Monique and her parents were together once again as they consoled her in the back of the limousine. The Ryans had never given her their approval, but on this day she could see that she'd finally received it. She laid her head on her mother's bosom, sobbing away, as the funeral procession journeyed to the burial place. Mr. Ryan tried desperately to remain stoic as he cleared his sinuses each time tears were about to flood his eyes. He reached over and held his daughter's hand, thinking how foolish he had been, but even more how regretful he was for not having known or accepted his grandson because of the color of his skin, a grandson many were pleased to embrace as their own.

*   *   *

A few days after Elijah was placed to rest, the Pope found himself strolling the halls of the Vatican. He was consumed by guilt and simply could not find the peace he once had. Moments later, he was back in his room staring at the same gun he had used to kill Elijah. He picked it up and pointed it in the center of his forehead. "Forgive me, my Lord," he said as he pulled the trigger that left him lying across the bed in a pool of blood.

Meanwhile, back in the United States, the president had resumed his hectic campaign schedule. Oblivious to the danger surrounding him, he walked toward the lectern after the mayor of Chicago completed the introduction. The audience cheered as the president's charismatic personality took a hold of them. At the top of a building across the street, a man lay on his stomach as he tried to steady his grip on the rifle he had aimed at the president's heart.

*   *   *

Three weeks later, Monique returned to the familiar beach of Santa Barbara where it all began. Walking with her head down, slowly kicking the sand, she bent and picked up one of the slippers that had fallen from her hands. She had aged gracefully and had become wiser from the experiences that time had taught her. Her beauty was intact, as some of her male counterparts were still admiring her as they jogged along the beach. She stopped and sat on the shore, looking out toward the ocean, remembering Sebastein and how much he too had loved the sea.

Suddenly she got up and put her hand above her eyes to keep the sun from her view. Now she could see clearly a little boy on a rock in the midst of the ocean, sitting calmly as several

214

white doves flew around his head, making a perfect circle. She looked right, then left, hoping she would see someone who could assist the little boy. But as she looked out toward the ocean again, the little boy was no longer there, only the doves, and then they began flying away one by one. Thinking that her eyes were playing tricks on her she smiled and slowly began to walk back home, a home that had held many pleasant childhood experiences for her, a place of refuge and sanctuary from life's tribulations, a place where she didn't have to hurry or feel sorry about anything.

At 11:30 P.M., Monique was sitting in the living room under the guise of watching television, but her thoughts were far away. Monique's reverie was interrupted when Mr. and Mrs. Ryan came in to say good-night. They were very worried about Monique, because she had said very little in the past week. Yes, they could understand being overcome by grief at the loss of one's son, but it seemed as if Monique was trying to give up on life. So Mr. and Mrs. Ryan used every excuse to check on her. They told her how good it was to have her home, hugged and kissed her, then said good-night.

Monique got up from the living room and went to the kitchen to get herself a cup of chocolate and a slice of home-made bread. On her way back to the living room she heard a noise coming from the basement. "Monique, my beloved," said a voice softly. Realizing that it was coming from the basement, she said, "Mom, Dad, is that you?" No answer. She bit the bread, holding it between her teeth as she tried to use the hand that was free to turn on the basement stairway's light. The light did not come on. Assuming that the bulb was blown, she continueᴅ to walk gingerly down the steps. She became a little alarmed as her name was constantly being echoed by the unfamiliar voice, which was rooted in the basement somewhere.

She got to the bottom of the stairs, fumbled her way to the switch to turn on the light, but it too was not working. "Is anyone down here?" she asked, becoming more frightened by the spookiness of the situation. She started to leave, realizing that the voice was no longer calling her name. "Old age is catching up with me," she said as she attempted to find her way back to the staircase.

"Why do you seek to leave when the time has finally come for us to be together," said a voice clearly.

"Okay, the joke is over. Who are you? This is not amusing," she said, shaking like a leaf in a hurricane. She spilled the hot chocolate on her hands. "Damn it," she said, looking toward the direction from where the voice was coming. "Who the hell are you? I am going to scream in the next four seconds if you don't identify yourself," she continued angrily.

Before she could finish her words, the darkness of the basement was penetrated by ten toes that illuminated a bright light from the sandals. She stepped back after observing what appeared to be two feet standing on their own, since the rest of the person's body was covered with darkness. Then slowly, from the bottom to top, the light unmasked the man from behind the shadows, being a part of, yet totally detached from, the light that beamed so brightly from the image of the individual who now stood in front of her. She held her mouth as the bread and chocolate fell to the floor. She kept stepping back, knocking over small furniture items as she tried to recover from the shock.

"Elijah, is that really you, my son, or is the devil playing a terrible trick on me?"

"Your eyes do not deceive, my beloved, but I am more than your son."

She started to move toward him but was startled by his erotic remarks.

"Oh, how I long to kiss you, to hold you and to make love to you, to feel the warmness of your body against mine. It's been so long now; we can be together once again."

"What has gotten into you? Who are you? You're not my son. My son would never speak to me in this manner."

"No, I'm not," said the image of Elijah as the light that was shining from him became dimmer and dimmer.

The basement was filled with darkness once again as a tiny glow of light found itself at the toes of the image of Elijah.

Then within a split second before the light could fade away, it gave birth to a huge and much brighter light that brought the entire basement out of darkness. Monique covered her face as she tried to see through her fingers, but it was no good. The light was too overpowering. Then the thunder began to make an old familiar sound in the heavens and lightning flashed repeatedly across the sky, almost as if it had found itself in the basement. She moved her hands from her face slowly as the image emerged from the light that eventually faded away in the background.

"Sebastein! My God, is that really you? Tell me my eyes are not deceiving me!"

"It is I, my beloved. As I have told you, with every death comes a new beginning."

She hesitated for a while but then slowly started walking toward him. The closer she got to him to confirm that she was not hallucinating, the more her body quivered. They walked slowly toward each other before rushing the final steps into each other's arms, squeezing each other so tightly that their bodies were almost one.

She kissed him passionately. "You came back to me just when they have taken away our son."

"My beloved, how can I make you understand, I am the son you bore. It was destined that you become the vessel that would allow me to fulfill the prophesy. Countless nights I lay awake in my room knowing that as Elijah your son I could never feel your body against mine."

"What are you saying? That you got me pregnant so that you could continue your life on Earth in order to do God's work? That I gave birth to you? That me having a son was all a lie? Why? Why in God's name would you do such a thing?" she asked angrily.

"How would you have reacted if I had asked you to allow me to continue life by being reborn through your womb. Would you have understood?"

Monique did not respond. She just stood there in shock, hoping that she was really having a bad dream. But this was no dream because Sebastein was standing before her in the flesh. Had she not just felt his body? *Maybe this is the beginning stages of going mad,* she thought.

"I know it is difficult to understand, but if I am to fulfill the prophesy, there will come another era when I must do this again."

"You mean you have done this before?"

"Yes, and I could not tell you the whole truth for the same reason Mary could not be told."

"And why is that?"

"Because it was forbidden by God." Sebastein leaned over and tried to kiss her but she stepped away from him. "Am I mistaken about what I am seeing in your heart? Do you not love me? Surely if the heavenly Father can forgive Lucifer for his transgressions, you can forgive me."

Monique turned her head and looked at her reflection in the mirror which was hanging on the wall to her right. "How can you still love me? I am more suitable to play the role of your mother than your wife. You're youthful and I am greying all over."

Before she could continue, Sebastein moved closer to her once again, reached behind her and unhooked her dress. Trembling in his arms, she watched him as he removed all her clothing. Slowly and gently he removed her barrette and watched her hair fall to her shoulder.

"What are you doing?" she asked as Sebastein took the hair and covered her entire face.

"I once told you that with every death comes a new beginning. Behold." He gripped both of her breasts in the palms of his hands, rested his cheek against hers and gently forced her head in the direction of the mirror. She stared at both of their renewed looks, a look that made them seem like a couple in their middle twenties. She went closer to the mirror, taking a better look. Then, without a word, she knelt down and wept at his feet.

Sebastein raised her to her feet, lifted up her hands to the heavens and said, "Father, behold my lover, my wife, and my mother. Help us that we may live in harmony as we all should fulfill our destiny, until it's time to die!"